Flowers of the Far Fields

Kelson Brewer

The following is a manuscript submitted to the
Clive Bros. Publishing Company, NY, under the
title:

Flowers of the Far Fields

by

James E. Torrey

*Accompanying documents have been included for
completeness and context. Publication pending.

Letter addressed to Marco Arwaldt from James Torrey
Dresden University, Germany: Mailbox 24
June 28, 1833

Dear Marco,

It is done. The story of the last three years of my life has been written down. It is so strange, now that I have reached the end, to come back to the beginning and see my first entries. I find it almost horrifically jarring, like going back in time to see oneself as a child and being blasted by both embarrassment and nostalgia at the same time. It is at this point of reflection where I realize that my dream, if I should even have called it that, has failed. An effort, maybe, is a better-fitting moniker. I'm no longer sure.

Though the scope of my original intention was immense, and my youthful zeal as intense as I have ever experienced, I find myself regarding it all with a level of pity. It seems so small, so superficial when emblazoned on the backdrop of the rest of my life.

When my journey ended, I deluded myself that it was not a failure, but simply done with; I harbored thoughts that I could cobble together the notes I had written in my journals and by some fierce and ruthless culling, produce a scientific work of some importance. This, I now understand, is not true. There is too much in my experience that I can't bear to see stricken from the final document. I had thought that the cold scalpel of higher education formed me into the perfect machine of scientific discovery and repose. But alas, I still leak oil all over the pages of my diaries.

In an effort to find solace for myself, my late mother, and the flowers, I have finished the manuscript. In truth, I can barely read it back to myself now. The chapters appear as abominable amalgams, containing the silly scientific names and pretentious verbiage of an inquiring journal along with the pitifully romantic musings of a young man experiencing the world for the first time.

Nevertheless, it is done. And, now that the dust has settled and the pencil shavings have been swept off my desk, there is only one matter left for this poor excuse of an introduction: that of dedication.

Though this journey is mine, it has also been that of the many people I have met on the way. Along with them, it has been the journey of the lilacs, the lilies, the grasses, and the buttercups as well. So, with the finalizing swipe of an ink-laden pen and the resignation that I am, and perhaps always have been, a better storyteller than a scientist, I write:

For Mother, for the friends, and for the flowers.

Introduction

My name is James Torrey. I am a botanist currently living in Black Hawk, Tennessee, on the cusp of the western frontier. This publication will be my first endeavor into the scientific realm of published literature, and though it may contain many personifying dialogues some might deem unfit for a scientific publication, I hope the reader will consider any unprofessional remarks or gestures as those of a scientist who loves his subject.

The study of specialized and rare botanical organisms is a criminally underrepresented science, even halfway through this nineteenth century, and it is for that reason I have decided to publish this, a foray into nature, in order that we may, as a whole, finally find and describe to others the rarest flowers in the known world.

As part of this introduction, I want to also include the reason for my enigmatic entrance into this profession, as it is near and dear to my heart. My mother owned a beautiful garden in my hometown of Black Hawk, and I have many fond memories of walking past its white picket fences and showing my many friends and peers her wonderful flowers. She would fill our yard with dahlias and rhododendrons, and even cover the giant grape trellises with various kinds of beautiful mosses and morning glories.

She kept up this marvel of my younger years all the way until her untimely death after my twenty-ninth birthday this past winter. During her life, she exhibited the utmost respect for her flowers, and I have no doubt this tenderness overflowed into her kind and accepting upbringing of myself.

I say my *many* friends and peers, but in truth I had few actual friends in my youth. Marco, my best friend from as far back as I can remember, also took an interest in my mother's lavish garden, and even studied botany with me at Porter's Hill University in our home state. I have never asked him if his superficial interest in our garden was what prompted his identical move to that specific realm of higher education, but I have a feeling it was.

Besides Marco, there was a young schoolgirl named Amy Willers; she would often work for my mother. We wasted many evening hours wandering through that matriarchal paradise, and in the little time she had before starting the housework, we went running under the trellises and past the rows of bulbous dahlia blooms. On occasion, I could distract both her and my mother by asking questions about the garden and prolong that time of peace before work had to be done, much to the delight of my young, boyish disposition.

*

This text will incorporate thorough descriptions and notes on six of the world's rarest flowering plants. I would like to dedicate my forthcoming expedition and its accompanying publication to my mother because of all she has done for me and my friends through the magic of her garden.

In her honor, I will begin this work by including an entry of one of her favorites: the lilac. The form of which will be repeated throughout. This will serve not only as an indulgence of sentimentality for me, the author, but also an example to you, the reader, of the framework of this text. Without further ado, I present the flowers of the far fields.

Letter addressed to Marco Arwaldt from James Torrey
London, UK
May 7, 1830

Marco,

I am bristling with excitement.

I have just finished the preliminary research on our six species for the coming months and can hardly contain myself. As I'm sure you have already guessed, this was rather a chore for me. In fact, they are so rare that there is not, as far as I can find, a single horticultural encyclopedia in print today that contains any of them in the proper categories, though you are much better at this detective work than I am.

I have also included a draft of the introductory chapter of the book. I have a feeling it will make you laugh. I decided to write it on my mother's lilacs. I even included you in it since this will remain between us anyway. I look forward to your edits. Please let me know what you think should be changed or modified in your next letter. If I have an idea of what is acceptable before heading out on my first trip, then it will be much easier to write adequately while away.

But back to my excitement: I have a lingering hope that the exclusive nature of the flowers might spike the interest of the general public in the fascinating and wonderful world of rare botany, and I have daydreams that, one day, the common American reader will have our book as a decorative piece of interest on their living room mantle, well-thumbed and annotated.

Being a writer as well as a botanist, I will undoubtedly feel compelled to share a small number of the stories that come along with such an ambitious undertaking. I'm sure there will be many. I feel that readers will enjoy these brief forays into my expeditious psyche, and my more scientific audience can always skip past these intermissions if the raw data is what they desire. I will be diligent in my scribing, and after all is said and done, I give you full permission to rein me in and tell me which extraneous details to exclude.

I hope, above all else, that I will be able to impart a similar inception of adventurous exhilaration through this, the publication of what will be, at its completion, my greatest achievement.

With my mother's death, her garden will never be the same, no matter how carefully I attempt to recreate it. However, her influence has been immortalized through you and me. That, at least, is a solace, don't you think?

Perhaps, through some prolonged form of vicarious creation, my garden of words can produce a similar effect for you and whoever else reads this if we ever get it published. I hope it does, even if it is but a fraction of the spring afternoons we were given by mother.

— J

1. The Lilac (*Syringa vulgaris*)

Location:

While it is clear that the flower originated from the Balkans and Ottoman Empire, the species quickly spread through the royal gardens of Babylon and Greece to the rest of eastern Europe, eventually landing in England sometime around the start of the seventeenth century. Today, lilacs have progressed even to American gardens, many thousands of miles from their native Illyrian Peninsula. Though originally thriving in montane habitats, lilacs have been shown to prosper in many varied climes, from the thrivent plains of the West to the rolling hills of England. Festivals are also held in Boston and New York to commemorate the flower. Thanks to the incredible work of Victor Lemoine, the plant is also richly celebrated in France. His influence has been so great on the plant that the special double-flowering cultivars have been colloquially called "French lilacs" in his honor.

Cultivation:

Today, the common lilac is grown decoratively in almost every corner of the globe. It is easy to acquire and care for, which has led to its popularity in settings ranging from homes, storefront window boxes, park trellises, courthouse plazas, and royal greenhouses. Additionally, the flower is also grown and sold for medicinal and aromatic purposes in nearly every major city on earth.

Description:

The term "lilac" refers to the Latin genus *Syringa* of which there are twelve known species. Lilacs grow as either trees or short shrubs ranging from two to six meters tall and have sweetly scented blooms. Their multistemmed bases have a light-gray bark that flakes with age. The blooms form in clusters of short, four-lobed flowers, each flower being three to four centimeters wide and blossoming in various shades of milky white to dark purple.

The species also grows a large array of light-green arrowhead leaves that surround the buds at the stem's terminus.

Personal Notes:

The trip to see lilacs has never been a long one. Even if my mother's lilacs were not thriving one year, the small central park of Black Hawk was always sure to have a bushel or two to the left and right of its naked grape trellis. More vibrant and lush than the municipal gardener's, my mother's lilacs were a constant companion waiting for me along the broken fence of my family's farm come early spring. Even today they hang over the road leading to our house, painting a pastel overtone to the reddening dirt road. I have kept them up ever since my mother's death, and I cannot help but sit with them awhile as my mind runs up and down the tree line that surrounds our property.

The wind blows gently past the one large tree in front of our house and rustles the buds one at a time, bobbing them cyclically up and down with its ebb and flow. As a child, it was often not enough to just observe them from the road. I had to get as close as I could and peer deeply at each little four-pointed star.

I distinctly remember an occasion on an early May afternoon while walking home from school with Amy. My family was not a poor one, and the chores that Amy often came over to help with were paid for handsomely. She was wearing a light-purple dress that hung just past her knees. Liberated by the spring air and the oncoming termination of school, she ran far ahead of me down our gravel lead.

I stopped to peer intensely at the lilacs, smelling the sweet aroma that had been absent for the past eight months. They progressed in age as you got closer to the house. The new, more peripheral bushes were tall and stout, and bloomed slightly later than their elderly neighbors. This left them with a thick furrow of closed buds wreathed with open ones, like pale-purple halos. On the other hand, the more elderly installations had significantly more powerful aromas. As you neared the house, the sweetened vanilla scent of the blooms closed in, curling all the way around you as you drew close to the end of the dirt road.

As I followed the row down the lane, I watched as the smooth bark of the young twigs slowly gave way to the grayish cracks of the old. Suddenly, a loud "BOO!" sent me sprawling into the gravel.

"Gotcha!" cried Amy, laughing as she helped me up. "Got to pay more attention out here in the wild. One of these days a bison's gonna come charging you down, and you'll be too busy sniffing flowers to notice."

I brushed the dust off my school uniform, a little peeved at being scared, but my anger diminished somewhat when I saw her eager, laughing face. We slowly continued walking. Just near the end, where the oldest lilacs pulsed in the prairie wind, I stopped one last time and put my face as close as I could to the flowers. I could feel the tiny star petals on my forehead. Amy, in a somewhat mocking manner, stuck her head next to mine.

"What are you looki—"

Barely had the words left her mouth when she let out a short, piercing scream and reeled back, tossing her head away from the bush and clawing her fingers through her blonde curls.

"What's wrong?" I asked, shocked and confused.

"A spider!" she shrieked at the bush before she ran down the lane to my front door. "A white one! The kind that will kill you!"

Unperturbed by her shock now that I had learned of its origin, I looked where her head had been. Sure enough, there hung a small, milky white spider, slowly spinning on a strand of silk from one of the lilac petals.

At that point in my life, I had no idea what it was called. I didn't even know its household name, let alone its scientific one. I remember entertaining myself at the time by envisioning that it had none, and was, by some incredible strain of luck, still undiscovered by science. *A lilac spider*, I thought. It had a beautifully pale body, almost velvety in its texture, giving it a soft appearance as opposed to the hostile shine or alien-like hairiness of other common spiders. Once it stopped spinning on its strand of web and tucked its legs out of view, it morphed almost magically into the image of a lilac petal.

I later learned from my mother that these were called white crab spiders, and though they were poisonous, their fangs were too short to pierce human skin. I smiled when she told me that. Amy may have "gotten me" many times over the course of our friendship, but my lilacs, at least that time, had gotten her back.

Despite my eventual understanding that these spiders had been found and categorized by scientists well before our chance encounter with them, the event served as a catalyst for my newfound interest in undiscovered species and linked that interest closely with my mother's garden. Of course, spiders no longer capture this particular desire of mine, but the idea that there may be a flower, perhaps lodged in between the barely visible crack of two monolithic slabs of a rock distantly removed from any civilization, that had not yet been discovered, threw my mind into a whirl of imagination and curious zeal.

After that day, I would sit up for hours at night simply conjuring up imaginary flowers in my mind. I imagined plants that ate insects and grew to meters in height and width. I created blooms that were so intoxicating they were used as bug repellant. My mind, spurred on by the untapped well of childish ideation, would rush over the plains of America, passing the reclusive rock faces and plateaus, continuing past the first settlements of New York, and crossing the great Atlantic. I followed the root systems of a fake species of flowering tree in Egypt before flitting hundreds of miles north to a yet undiscovered species of red sunflower in Italy.

My studies have only strengthened this imaginative excitement. To this day, my mind still races from continent to continent, gliding through forests and valleys like a bird. Today, my body will follow it, and it's bringing a notebook and pencil along.

Letter addressed to James Torrey from Marco Arwaldt
Black Hawk, TN, USA
July 15, 1830

Dear James,

I am irreducibly happy for your excitement. It pains me not to be able to accompany you, but my occupation has, as usual, been a stalwart blockade to my personal freedom. Nonetheless, I have checked over your notes and believe everything is as ready as it can be.

I wish you luck. Make sure to catch your ships on the correct dates. I must also warn you that your first quarry has not a small chance of taking quite some time. I pray you will not be frustrated by this. I have been informed by locals in the area that the flower we located is "close" to its bloom, but such things, as you know, are quite nebulous in botany. Of course, I have accounted for this possibility in your travel plan, which you have a copy of, but patience may be your greatest asset for this particular adventure.

If anything goes awry, please contact me as soon as you can. I will always be available for your letters.

— MA

Letter addressed to Marco Arwaldt from James Torrey
London, UK
September 20, 1830

Dear Marco,

I have had the most fascinating trip! As you know, the boat you booked for me, the St. Silas, left on the sixteenth. I am writing this passage on that very vessel as it plunges eastward, and what an adventure I have already had.

I traveled on various ships when I went to South America for my botanical thesis, and this trip has proven summarily identical to my previous ones. This is, I suppose, a testament to the calibration of modern transport. The sailors and other passengers of the St. Silas have also proven excellent company, though slightly obsessed with the games of poker and euchre, respectively.

I told one of the cooks that I was a botanist from America, and with silent delight (he rarely spoke, even to the sailors he seemed close to and worked with) he ran straight to the crew's quarters and returned in only a few seconds, holding out a tiny pink peony bud. I was astonished, as it looked like it had been expertly preserved through some sort of mummification.

Proud that he had impressed a botanist, he gladly answered my questions using his usual various mime gestures and written symbols, which he scribbled on a dirty piece of paper he readily produced from his overall pocket. From this rather odd interaction I was led to believe that the peony had been a gift from his late grandmother, and that he kept it with him wherever he went. I inquired as to its preservation, but the language barrier proved too great, and I could not understand his answer. I'm sure you would have loved the specimen if you could have seen it. After about an hour's worth of inquiry, I finally took my leave of him with my condolences as to the death of his grandparent. To my surprise, he grinned giddily and communicated to me that it was all right, for she had died just under fifteen years ago, in 1816.

*

Our planned route should take the best part of this month and the next, but I have already passed the bulk of it quickly with the help of my new sailor friends and the botany books I brought with me. I fear I will not even be able to finish the second one before we arrive at our destination: the Port of Belawan. I will send this letter from the port office when I arrive there. I must admit, I'm a little nervous that it will not reach you, but I can do little more than cross my fingers and hope at this point. I will send you word when my prey is caught, and I am out of the forest.

— J

2. The Corpse Flower (*Amorphophallus titanum*)

Location:

The corpse flower has only ever been observed to grow in a small equatorial corner of Sumatra, where it often sprouts from cracks in the many limestone deposits of the island's western rainforests. While it is possible that the plants grow in other similar but undiscovered climes around the world, none have been observed. Currently, Sumatra should be seen as the sole natural location of the *Amorphophallus titanum* (or titan arum).

Cultivation:

The history of the cultivation of the corpse flower is shrouded in mystery. To date, multiple botanical gardens have claimed to possess seeds of the plant and have subsequently attempted separate cultivations, none of which have been officially documented. It is said that in July of 1827, the Kew Gardens attempted the growth of a single flower. This was followed the next year, in September, by rumors that the Royal Gardens in Belfast had attempted a similar feat. Finally, there have been reports of three separate translocation attempts made by the botanists at the University of Kensington in the latter part of this year. All of these attempts have unfortunately failed to produce adequate growth, and the complete, natural life of the *Amorphophallus titanum* remains entirely endemic to the East Indies.

Description:

The *Amorphophallus titanum* is the largest flowering plant in the world. In its flowering phase, its appearance is characterized by a massive conical column called a spadix surrounded by a single, massive, leaf-like structure called a spathe. The spadix, during bloom, is usually a yellow or light green hue and can reach up to a towering 3.3 meters tall. The underside of the spathe is a similar color to the column. However, as the flower blooms, the spathe reveals that it is actually a single deep-red petal, similar in form to the popular calla lily, though obviously much larger.

From the outside, the entire plant appears to be one large flower bloom, but hidden from view by the spathe, the spadix is actually surrounded by two thin rings of additional small blossoming flowers, one on top of the other. The top ring contains the male flowers, while the bottom contains the females. During bloom, the rings open in cycles, with the top ring blooming first and the bottom ring following about a day later; this allows the males to pollinate the females accordingly. During this pollination, additional pollen is released through the spadix and is often carried by the wind to other members of the same species within its sphere of influence.

The rather macabre name of the flower comes primarily from its odor and color during bloom. The end of the spadix, which is the primary vehicle of volatilization, is also very warm during the end of its growth cycle and regularly reaches temperatures of 90–98 degrees Fahrenheit, close to human body temperature. Its fragrance closely resembles that of carrion or rotting flesh, and the deep red color of the spathe adds to its unsettling presence. It is clear, however, that these characteristics, while rather offensive to humans, attract a large amount of scavenging insects such as beetles and flesh flies, which aid the plant in pollination. Underground, the plant's corm, or stem, is also the largest in the world, reportedly weighing around one hundred pounds or more on its own.

Its bloom is not well documented, but during an observation in 1825, the opening lasted for only forty-three hours before the beginning phases of wilting set in. The spathe is purported to open around evening, and its blooming fragrance grows in strength until around the middle of the night. It is believed that this rather oppressive aroma signals the female blooms' openness to pollination. The plant's spathe usually collapses first when wilting begins, which starts about halfway through the blooming process. It should be noted that cultural observation should be taken with a sparse amount of confidence, as public findings are difficult to substantiate.

Personal Notes:

I have mentioned my good friend Marco Arwaldt in the introduction, and it is with a light heart that I have accepted his help in planning these journeys of mine. While he did go to Porter's Hill for botany originally, he actually finished with a degree in international business (a specialization that terrifies me to no end). I believe his once expansive knowledge of botany has slowly trickled through the cracks over the course of his studies, but he has become somewhat of a luminary in his new profession. His ability to find people in the world is unmatched, and his newly realized talent with languages (he now fluently speaks thirteen of the most widely used, so many that I forget which ones he knows by heart and which ones he is currently studying) has given him the ability to impress even more people with the characteristic brilliance that has so enlivened our lifelong friendship. We have remained friends quite easily outside of school thanks to our frequent correspondence by letter, of which I have a mountain sitting in my records cabinet. These include anything from small life updates to academic dialogues pages in length. His stories, due to the rather exciting nature of his profession, have always outshone mine by leaps and bounds. But being the incredible friend he is, he has inevitably found ways to inquire about the almost embarrassingly simple goings-on in my life:

"Oh, is the post really that slow in Tennessee? What a horror of an organization. I wonder how it could be improved."

"What day did you say Mrs. Malone got married again? I can't seem to find the note in my files, and I would love to send them a letter of congratulations."

"You really ought to come to London soon, James. The Lynn Art Festival is coming up this spring, and I have a feeling you might enjoy some of the rather marvelous floral exhibits."

Who knows, perhaps this monumental undertaking of mine will finally give him the same excitement that his fascinating stories give me.

He also frequently inquires about my mother's house, a property with which he is deeply familiar. His house was just about half a mile west of mine, so during the winter, he commonly walked with me after school. The cold got to us quickly, as the western winds were always chilled from their glides over the sliding prairie, and the memories I have of us sprinting to the kitchen stove for warmth are countless.

One particular evening stands out in my memory, as it is emblematic of Marco's curious and brilliant nature. I will relate it here as a sort of resumé for my partner, though I'm sure he will tell me to omit this section in the future.

*

We had just arrived after the harrowing walk. We knocked the dirt off our boots before slipping out of them and stepping through the wooden door into the kitchen. I used what we had to make two cups of hot chocolate, a customary drink after school, and was just about to lay them on the counter and call Marco over when his voice rang out from the adjacent dining room.

"James, I have something to show you." I could hear the smile in his voice, and quickly set the steaming cups down and followed his invitation.

He was standing in the corner of the room, observing one of my mother's decorative displays of dahlias. My mother often brought inside the most beautiful blooms she could find from her garden just before the bitter cold of the western winter descended on Black Hawk. The flowers could last a little longer under her supervision that way. She was always careful to hydrate them with lukewarm water from the stove, place them in well-ventilated areas, and tend to them every day. These vases were usually set up in the kitchen, and I was surprised to see that one had been moved into this room in particular. This area had no natural sunlight and was not, I thought, suitable for the longevity of the flowers.

"Come here," said Marco, waving me over to him. "I knew I was right."

The thing he had called me over to see was readily apparent to my eager eye. The flowers were in surprisingly excellent condition. It was nearly two weeks after the first cold spell of the year, and their colors had not even started to fade. The edges of the petals were holding firm, which, I noticed, was a stark difference compared to the ones still in the kitchen.

Marco was studying my expression carefully. When he saw my realization turn slowly to slight confusion, he began his explanation.

"You didn't notice, but I moved this here a week ago. You and your mom will have to forgive me for taking that liberty, but it was worth it in the end. I noticed the flowers in your kitchen were starting to wilt rather early. With all the care your mother gives these decorations, I would have expected them to last at least half a month more, and I got an idea. Here, let me show you."

He then walked back into the kitchen. I followed.

"You see, it's your fruit bowl . . . it has to be." He pointed at the blue and gray bowl at the corner of our counter, still filled with a few pears and apples left over from the summer stockpile we had accrued.

"The vases that wilt have always sat right above the fruit bowl. I noticed it when the flowers on the far side of their respective vases seemed to be slightly less wilted than their identical, but conversely placed siblings. I tested this first by rotating the vases at the beginning of last month and was rewarded by seeing their condition start to mirror that of the originals after about a week. So, I naturally found the least wilted of the bunch and relocated it to the spot that you just saw, away from the fruit bowl, and voilà!"

He punctuated his triumphant explanation with a snap of his fingers and positively beamed at the fruit bowl before us. He then continued.

"There must be some kind of gas that comes off of ripening fruit that induces a similar aging effect in their growing neighbors, although I'll admit I haven't the slightest way to prove that to you. But all the same, I'd bet my last dollar that the flowers I've separated will last twice as long as these sorry fellows."

"I'll take your word for it," I replied with a laugh, and I did. To this day, I have never placed a vase of flowers next to a fruit bowl, and they do inevitably and invariably color the room for weeks into the winter months.

*

I hired Marco in my current endeavor to find me a guide to take me from the port into the forest where I was to meet a company of monks at their temple. They would, I was told, let me stay at their place of worship until it was time to lead me to the flower. These monks had spotted the plant almost two decades ago and had reportedly witnessed it bloom every four years almost exactly to the day. To be absolutely sure I would see it, I had prepared enough money and resources to stay at the site for up to a year if needed.

*

After stepping off the ship with my belongings, I was at once met with my guide. She was a young woman about twenty or so years old. The dark skin of her face shone in the harsh afternoon sun, and she shook my hand vigorously. She was wearing a headscarf that covered her forehead and neck along with a matching dress, both made of a thick brown material.

"My name is Anisa. I will guide you," she said in very good English. "I understand you study the flowers, right?"

I replied that I did, and that she was leading me to one of the rarest in the world.

"Oh?" she said with a tilt of her head. "Is it really that rare?" She laughed and told me she had seen it all her life, and that, in her opinion, it was a rather unpleasant thing to travel across the world for. This idea made me laugh as well, and we were soon on our way to being friends. Her surprise at the conviction of my journey was at first absurd to me, but quickly I realized that it would be equally absurd if she had shown up at my door and said she had traveled more than twenty thousand miles to see my mother's lilacs.

Her smile, which showed an unusual—but oddly perfect—set of slanted teeth that made her upper lip curl when she grinned, was striking when compared to the leering grins of the sailors I had grown accustomed to in the past couple of months. Her head wrapping covered her hair and neck, but I felt like I could see all of who she was and what she thought in that smile. The openness of her character shone contrastingly next to my naturally reserved nature, and the men passing us as they unloaded the ship looked positively dull and secretive in comparison. As we exited the port area and walked out onto the street, she hailed a horse-drawn cart, and we got in and started riding through the large city of Medan.

The road was poorly maintained. The cart rocked back and forth with the winding street, sometimes jolting from side to side as the slender wheels hit cracks in the compacted dirt roadway. One jolt was so vicious that I was almost thrown off the side, but I was thankfully caught by Anisa. I hung there by my coat collar, awkwardly scrabbling for a handhold to lever myself back up to safety. It was only after I had scrambled back into my seat that I realized Anisa was surprisingly strong for how young she looked. I was a slight man, but had played secondary school sports and run through the trails around my university when I had time during my schooling days. She was easily stronger, and I'm sure could outwork me at almost any activity. Luckily, she let my near-fall pass without acknowledging it, and we talked lightly about the town together for the rest of the trip.

I was aware that the Port of Belawan was in the northern part of the island, and that the corpse flower was endemic to the western rainforests, but when I inquired about the length of the journey, Anisa replied that it was "very close, only a day's ride from the house."

The house in question was hers, and she lived there with three other women. I was given something to eat after arriving: a marvelously warm bowl of noodle soup that tasted faintly of carrots, peas, and eggs, and which was served with copious amounts of bread and rice. It was more than I could finish. I was fed in my room; it seemed like eating together was not a custom in this house, or at least not with guests, as I faintly heard the women talking and eating down the hallway. Before I finished, however, there was a knock at my door.

I got up to meet my visitor. It was Anisa again. She was looking shyly at the floor and held her hands behind her back, still dressed in her brown head wrap and long day dress.

"Good evening," I said rather clumsily, not really sure what to say. The coquettish look disappeared from her face, replaced by a sly, mocking smile as her eyes lifted up from the ground. Silently she pulled her right hand from behind her back and opened her palm. In her hand were three white coffee flowers. The smile remained and widened, curling her lip again. She looked as if she had tricked me in some way or successfully executed a prank.

"You are a man of flowers, right?" She asked with that pretty, crooked grin. "These are our flowers!" She tilted her hand as a gesture, and after I quickly cupped my hands together in response, she let the white petals tumble into my palms.

Her mouth closed again, and she looked up straight into my surprised eyes.

"What a funny thing, isn't it, a man who likes flowers so much?" And with that, she ran away down the hallway, saying "Goodnight!" over her shoulder as she left.

I stared blankly at the newly vacant hallway for a moment. The flowers were fresh and smelled of magic. I had actually never seen coffee flowers in person before. Each bud had five thin alabaster petals that stood out in a star formation. In each gap sprouted the flower's long, jagged stamens, which were skinny and knife-like. From the center sprung a long, pale pistil. The whole thing together resembled the tiny reaching fingers of a child's outstretched hand.

She must have picked them while harvesting the coffee fruit earlier that day or the day before. They couldn't have been more than twenty-four hours old. I made a note that, if I were ever to see the *St. Silas* again, I should ask the mute cook if he could find a way to preserve the coffee flowers just like his grandmother's peonies.

*

We left early in the morning on horse, traveling slowly through the countryside. Sumatra was beautiful. The flat, dusty city quickly gave way to the greenest hills I had ever seen. They looked woolen and soft under the cover of thick, mossy vegetation, and the rolling slopes of the island's outer terrain fell straight like whetstone slabs into the rumbling azure carpet of the surrounding sea. The forests, supported by massive walls of limestone and granite, lent themselves to the formation of long, thin waterfalls, and you could see small strips of acid-white water slither their way down the distant hills. My short stint in South America was nothing compared to this newfound natural liberty, and a part of me wished the temple was more than a day's ride away. The air was warm, and the montane breeze brushed past us on its way through the valleys.

There were many, many plants that I had never seen before, and I had no shortage of questions for Anisa about the names and characteristics of the local flora. The trees closest to the trail were called *Knema* trees and were short and puffy. They had small spade-like leaves with glistening, reflective surfaces; the leaves fanned out and were ringed by orange, acorn-shaped buds. At night, these buds would open and reveal a bright red cherry on the inside.

I also encountered a rather surprising species of tree near the edge of the village: conifers. I could hardly believe my eyes when, after inspecting their skinny, similarly reflective leaves, I discovered the namesake conical seeds hanging underneath their branching canopies. The seeds' resemblance to the pinecones I used to throw around the yard in my youth was striking, and the welcome wash of nostalgia that came reminded me of home.

As we were ascending out of a densely packed valley, a flash of color caught the corner of my left eye. Stopping my horse, I saw that the hue came from a peculiar-looking flower growing out of a crack in the rock. It hung earthward out of the crack by a thin, almost filamentary stem, but quickly curved upward and widened into a single bulbous, tubular petal. The jar-shaped bloom had a vibrant, speckled-red coloring that covered its entire exterior.

"What is this, Anisa?" I asked, stopping our progress and getting off my horse to get a closer look, in awe of the strange plant. Ahead of me, she stopped her ride and looked around. The horse's head curled back too, mimicking her.

"Oh, you found a monkey cup!" she said with a grin. "There are tons of them around, although red ones like that are hard to find."

"I'm—I don't think I've ever heard of such a thing . . . it's . . . well, fantastic. Actually, I'm not sure anyone's ever recorded this before. They are normal, you say?"

In answer, she laughed. "Yes, quite normal. I see them every day on the way to the river near town. You will see many more by the time we arrive at the temple. All shapes and sizes." With that, she turned back around, her horse's head again following like a puppet on a string.

Seeing her about to leave, I jumped back on my horse, giving the flower one last longing look as we pressed on. I had the nagging feeling that the "monkey cup" had yet to be officially recorded. I surely would have remembered its shape in my studies. But, as her horse trotted onward up the trail, I resolved to leave it, and took a mental note to search for its taxonomy when I got back to America.

As we crested the hill, the tree line broke for thirty meters or so where a loose shale-like rock covered the mountainside. The gap revealed the sprawling breadth of the rainforest we had just woven through. In the distance, a wide black mountain loomed in what seemed like the center of the island. I had not been able to see it from the ground due to the densely packed *Knema* branches, but once I was standing in the sloped clearing, I could view its hulking figure with an uneasy clarity.

The mountain was markedly less vegetative than the ones surrounding it. While it was still tinted green, it was darker and deeper in hue. As my eyes traveled down its form, I noticed that a massive swathe of forest was cut out, widening a cone of treeless expanse down to its base, which fell out of sight.

"That is Mount Tambora," said Anisa, following my gaze. "In 1815, when I was a little girl, the mountain erupted and killed many people."

I noticed that her gaze, too, was fixed on the sable slope, and her right hand tightly clenched her reins. She said that even though it was far away from her village, many of the people she knew had died after the explosion in the aftermath of dust and ash. The air was contaminated for a long time after the initial tragedy, and that made it difficult to breath. Hundreds of people all over Sumatra died from lung disease due to the toxic volcanic fumes.

"The ash looked like clouds at first." She spoke in a far-off tone with the stressed forehead of someone trying hard to remember something. "You could see them lower over everything in the morning. At the beginning of the night, when the sun set, the smoke turned the sky and everything below red."

I was shocked that she would mention something so terrible to a stranger. During the year she mentioned, I would have been only fourteen. After another moment of quiet thoughtfulness, she turned her horse away from the outlook and back toward the trail. Silently, we continued on our journey.

Besides small explanations of the landscape, we did not talk much after, but it was the full, comfortable silence that happens to fall on a situation when conversation is no longer needed. The omnipresent atmosphere of the Sumatran jungle filled the space between the distant hiss of crashing waterfalls and our horses' footsteps. My confusion at the introduction of the Mount Tambora topic quickly faded away as well, and it was replaced by a strong feeling of connectedness. I was experiencing all of Sumatra, even her tragedies, and by the time night began to fall, I felt like I had seen, smelled, and heard the entire history of the island.

We rode for almost eighteen hours straight, stopping just once to feed the horses and eat. Despite this, neither of us were that tired. We both wanted to make it to our destination before sunrise. I was excited and hurried my horse more than I probably should have. This would constantly position me too close to Anisa's mount, but she masterfully sped up and slowed down to maintain a comfortable distance.

The blackness settled through the trees, and I remember wishing I could have seen the sunset at that moment. We were riding southward across the sloped ridges of the island at the time, and the viciously sloped mountains to the west blocked our view of the horizon. This also threw us into a blanket of shade quite early in the evening, and the contrast between the darkness of the ground at my feet and the bright vividness of the looming mountains made my eyes hurt. I had not brought a hat to block the rays and was soon regretting my decision. Anisa, with her scarves, didn't seem to be bothered at all.

As the night grew darker and darker, I again started to worry. I had also not brought a lamp to guide my way, and I was about to ask Anisa whether we should stop before we fell off a cliff when the moon finally broke over the eastern oceanic horizon.

The Sumatran moon is titanic in its presence. So bright was its beam of light that it drowned out the stars around it. The dust circling our horses was framed in thick bands of luminescence just like during the day, and they formed pale ghostly shards that intersected the ground like spears of glowing crystal. It was clear that no lamp was needed. We continued our journey into the forest, my questions and anxieties evaporating into the air, drifting behind me in the night.

My excitement started to build again, and Anisa told me that the monks usually made coffee at the temple and would gladly share it with us. When we passed the sixteen-hour mark and the slow swell of fatigue started to take hold of me, the idea of a steaming-hot cup spurred me through the waxing hours of the morning.

*

At around five o'clock, we burst through the final fence of overgrown rainforest, and our horses trod gratefully into a wide grass-covered clearing. A dirt road led to the structure at the center of the emerald dell. It was much larger than I had expected and built almost entirely out of a bright red brick. The whole building consisted only of a single giant, layered pyramid, with four vertical pillars, one at each end. The brickwork could be seen through a veil of moss and vines that crept their way through the crevices of the structure, as if dragging it into the grass below. With the amber sun rising behind it, the building's shadow stretched far in front.

I gazed at it for a good minute, my horse continuing to trot forward, before I realized Anisa had stopped.

Looking back, I asked what she was doing.

"Time for me to go. They are expecting you, the scientist, not me." I was struck with a pang of strange panic and was stuttering my indignation when she leapt off her horse and pulled a roll of paper from one of her saddlebags. She then walked over to my horse's side and held the paper up to show me. She angled it to catch the rays of the rising sun, and I was able to see that it was a map of Sumatra.

"Here is where we came," she said, pointing to a trail marked in red ink, talking over my stuttered objections. "You will find it and remember, don't worry." Then, she smiled up at me and silently pushed it into my hands. "I'm sorry," she finished, and before I could say anything, she had whirled herself back on her horse, flying shawl and all, and turned back to the trail.

"Wait," I said, softer than I meant to.

Looking over her shoulder and smiling at my awkward bewilderment, she yelled back, "Take some coffee seeds back with you. Grow some Sumatra in America."

I faltered in my reply and stood there for just a few moments more, staring at the horse and its rider as they grew smaller and smaller before disappearing through the veil of trees. I did not have the breath or heart to tell her that coffee did not grow in the shadeless soil of the Tennessee plains.

*

The Buddhists' coffee was incredible. Coffee in America is usually roasted in large metal rolling roasters, where every bean is heated to almost the exact same temperature. The monks, obviously lacking such a convenience, roasted the beans in a large flat pan over a fire. The result was a shockingly delicious and inconsistent roast. It almost tasted flowery, like vegetables. I was told that they usually drank the potion before meditation to help them focus. I decided to take it for breakfast.

The monks were a kind and easygoing people who spent most of their days praying and meditating. I was given food and coffee for every meal. The temple itself almost expanded as you entered it, and I happily spent many days exploring the jagged architecture of its interior and the various flowers that surrounded the magnificent structure. Out of the cracks in the stonework budded countless purple oriental lilies, their deep-hued centers ringed by bright white edges and stiff green stalks. Also in abundance was the Arabian jasmine, which one of the monks told me was called *melati*. It grew in long clumped bushes that smelled of sweet sugar. The smooth white flowers popped out in whorled cups and were picked in the mornings to make tea.

Though the inhabitants of this jungle temple were incredibly hospitable, I did not have the same kind of friendship with them that I had instantly felt with Anisa. I convinced myself that this was fine, as I had work to do, even if the work at present was only to wait.

It took only two months. On the third day of the first week of December, I was informed by my guides that the time had come; a scout had already been out to the spot where the *A. titanum* grew. It was ready for us. Our party had everything packed in two hours, and by the afternoon we had started our hike into the forest.

We made the trek without horses, and I became quickly aware of the difficulty in carrying all my notation supplies by myself. The journey did, however, give me more time to admire the rainforests of the island. We were lucky, and it did not rain the whole day. There had been a camp set up near the bloom in preparation for my visit, and I marveled at both the kindness of the Sumatran people and the uncanny detail in Marco's preparations. The corpse flower is said to only bloom at night, and the whole day I was shaken by tremors of excitement and anticipation at the coming dusk. My chest also tightened with a small amount of fear. Most of my botanical observation had taken place in American greenhouses, where blooms and pollination lasted for a whole season, not a few hours, because they were artificially prolonged by the careful hands of gardeners and curators. Nonetheless, I had confidence in my education, and spurred on by the idea that such a close observation of the corpse flower had never been attempted before by an outsider, I walked briskly through the dense vegetation, only steps behind my guides.

I also initially wondered at the size of my traveling party. The monks were not exactly talkers, and I felt a little awkward being flanked by four other men on what I had assumed would be a semi-solitary expedition of one or two members at most. Soon though, it became evident that these companions carried much-appreciated conveniences. One carried only a lamp and enough oil to last three nights if needed. Another carried food for the group and was an expert at preparing the correct amount to keep the party going. The third had brought a machete and various bags to hang food off the wet ground at night, away from the animals and bugs of the soil. I had been under the impression that the machete would be used to clear the vegetation in front of us, but the monk stayed at the back, and I was soon made aware that the knife was not for clearing stationary organisms, but for protecting against mobile ones. Such an idea scared me when I thought of it, and I often found myself looking over my shoulder and listening closely to the many hisses and whispers of the forest. The fourth monk helped me carry my load of supplies, which I now found embarrassingly overzealous compared to that of my companions. The fourth was also the guide; he was an old man with an incredibly long face and an uncomfortably upright posture who I was told had found the flower on a walk almost a decade before.

It was late afternoon when we finally arrived, and there it was.

The plant, cocooned into a magnificent green pod, stood more than three meters tall. The veins of the single massive petal stood out as the bloom wrapped itself tightly around the velvety green spadix. I could barely contain my excitement. Three meters looked so small written on the pages of a botany book, but what stood before me now was a monster of an organism. It was as if a leathery green bear was standing motionless on its hind legs, stuck in the perpetual stance of preemptive attack and domination. I could see the bleeding red tinge around the edge of the cusped petal, signaling its transition into bloom. The spadix, round and almost phallic-looking, added to its off-putting nature.

To my surprise, I could not smell anything, but when I brought this concern to the guide monk, he chuckled, tilting his head to look at the pinnacle of the green spire. At the end of his laugh, he touched the bulbous petal with one hand and said only one word in English:

"Wait."

*

It took only a day. The next evening, I was preparing my sleeping cot near the trail when I caught a whiff of the foulest stench I had ever smelled in my life. It was like a combination of rotting flesh, feces, and sugary alcohol. The smell was pungent and strong, and it soon became omnipresent throughout our camp, seeping like a syrupy fog into every nook and cranny of my tent. Thrilled by this, I quickly left my previous duty of gathering kindling for a fire and approached the pillar of a plant.

Sure enough, the petal had slowly begun to unfurl, exposing the worm-colored skin of its inner layer. I cannot describe the experience adequately in writing, but it was as if the plant held dominion over the whole area. Its titanic presence was expanded atmospherically by its vibrating aroma. Whatever the scent touched belonged to the gigantic, magnificent obelisk, and it sat like an effigy of some floral god that expanded its eminence invisibly across the forest. The smell, the monks said, spread for miles during bloom, attracting as much attention from the surrounding carrion bugs as possible. And bugs there were. Flies surrounded its tall spadix like a black halo, and members of some strange species of blue-black beetle could be seen crawling up its stem. As we walked around camp, we had to make sure not to step on the wriggling river of insects that made pilgrimage to the bloom, encircling it in a spiral of legs and wings.

The plant lay to the left of a narrow trail along a sloped embankment, which was perfect for observation. I could witness its unraveling petal from the trail below, and when needed, I could walk up the slope of the hill and look into its cavernous maw from which the spadix protruded. Within four hours, the petal had fully opened, and the entirety of the flower could be seen from above. I walked up the hill, grabbing on to the slippery trees of the embankment with my uphill hand; the lantern monk followed close behind, holding the lamp on a long pole to give me light. I wanted to see for myself the rings of the smaller flowers on the inside, a description of which I had ravenously searched for in any textbook on the subject but failed to find. The two rings, though known about from dead specimens, had never been scientifically observed in bloom, the reason mostly being their invisibility from the outside. The *A. titanum* was already barely known to the scientific world, and observation of the flowers would normally require cutting a hole in the outer petal, preemptively stopping an already short bloom and killing the legendary plant. But, with my high vantage point granted by the grace of natural chance, I peered into the chasm of the opening flower bud.

I saw them, grotesque in their alien-like appearance. The two rings, attached directly onto the central spadix, were situated on top of each other and only centimeters away from the base of the plant. The male flowers resembled the yellow kernels of American corn and formed a skin-crawling hive approximately seven centimeters wide. Even more horrifying were the female buds. Situated directly below the males, the females each had a tiny round red bulb jutting out from the milky yellow underbelly of the spadix. Tiny black spore-like stalks topped with round white orbs sprouted from each red bulb. Each of these stalks, unearthly in their appearance, curved upward toward the light of my lantern, and I could see the hair-like fibers of the orbs, ready to receive the pollen of their higher brethren.

"Watch," said the lantern monk beside me, and with a grin, he lifted the lantern above the titan arum and slowly wafted it above the spadix. The lantern itself was vented at the top and bottom, and as he jockeyed it with the long staff, the flame began to flicker violently as it passed over the top of the flower. After the third or fourth pass, it blew out completely, leaving a wisp of smoke that quivered with the *A. titanum*'s noxious breath. We were plunged into darkness, and he let it stay that way for a moment, leaving only the crushing weight of the vapors floating around our heads. Then, after almost a minute of silent night, he struck a match once more, and relit the lamp before we descended.

The whole experience was otherworldly, and after a minute or two, I had to draw back and take a breath. Quickly, I descended to camp and wrote furiously in my notes. This process was repeated all throughout the night. I flew back and forth between the slipperiness of the slope and the light of my tent, gathering measurements, writing descriptions, and taking in the magic of the largest flower in the world. My buzzing industriousness lasted all the way until morning.

*

We stayed until the bloom closed, a process that only took about thirty-two hours. As the first cracks of sunlight peered in through the thick hanging foliage on the second day of our observation, the wilting had already begun. By the time the warm dawn crawled its way through the obscured horizon to the foot of my tent, the red top of the petal could no longer be seen. The spadix had collapsed. The greenish-purple leaf had already turned a pale brown, and this was enough to dissipate the intangible aura that had surrounded the flower the night before. In surreal fashion, the spell that the monolithic flora had cast over our camp, and over however many kilometers such a magic could spread, slowly vanished, sucking itself back into the dying flower with the lethal sunrise. I felt the weight of the situation lift off my shoulders. My notes had been taken; my scientific data collected. But even with this feeling of accomplishment, I felt sad to see the flower wilt so easily and so soon. In a way, it felt like a small god of the forest had died in front of me, and its idol, the only corporeal manifestation of its power, was now to be overcome with moss and bugs and lay dormant for another few years, sleeping in the coffin of its fading aroma.

*

The trip back seemed much shorter than the expedition out. My bags were lighter due to there being less food in them, and the plunder that I left with—the information scribbled into my notebooks—weighed nothing. Though I had hardly returned to the temple, my mind was already at my writing desk again, compiling everything I had discovered into the beginning of my new book. The monks' farewell was as warm as their welcome, and they left me well equipped for my day's ride back to the port. That trip, with its shining brilliance and quiet progress, was one of the best experiences of my life. As I pushed my horse through the green leaves of the encroaching ferns, I could embrace that fleeting feeling of accomplishment that comes with a finished job. The sun shone blissfully between the competing canopies of the overhanging jungle, and I felt the peace that one only experiences when ripped from the bustling city of modern life. No carriages, no farm duties, no thesis papers to get approved; just the forest, the security of having a journal full of notes tightly tied to my saddle, and the steady trot of the trip out of the rainforest.

Letter addressed to Marco Arwaldt from James Torrey
Gloucester, UK
No date given

Dear Marco,

Sumatra was otherworldly, and my hands shake as I recall these memories again. I fear that in my excitement, my writing will come across as sensational instead of scientific, but I cannot withhold the glorious effect that this trip has had on me. It's as if I had been searching for the fountain of youth and I am returning with a vial of livelihood in my pocket. You will no doubt be surprised at how soon I am back. What we thought might take over a year has only taken four months, and this, in my eyes, frees up some needed space for research or preparation. I will, however, leave most of that up to you, as it is out of my depth. Set me in a direction, friend, and I will start marching.

The ship I found is heading first to Xiamen, China and should be there in less than a month. Of course, this letter might take just as long, so I will wait for your reply at the port office. Lodging in the port district is at least one thing I can manage on my own.

Letter addressed to James Torrey from Marco Arwaldt

Port of Xiamen, China

January 30, 1831

It is good to hear from you, James.

These preliminary notes you included are fascinating, and I must admit I am quite impressed with the sheer size of this plant. The experience must have been incredibly rewarding for you. I'm glad.

The brevity and direction of your journey is also a boon of sorts, as I was having trouble finding you adequate passage to Xiamen for your next flower during the summer. This does bring a couple of complications or opportunities, depending on the way you look at it.

In five months' time, there is a ship called The Solidarity that is leaving Xiamen for New York. This is a fishing vessel, and has no passenger seats, but the clerk has assured me that such accommodations can materialize themselves with the proper credentials. We are lucky, it seems, as it appears I happen to have friends in the right places, and I have sent a letter reserving a room on the ship if you are willing to take it. This will mean you stay in Xiamen to look for your second specimen and leave for home in early June.

Of course, this is incredibly short notice, so I have gone ahead and booked you the room, but if you decide such a turnaround is too quick for you, feel free to send a letter to the port clerk in New York informing them, and I will smooth things out afterward. If you do happen to accept, however, send me a letter and I will ship some supplies by the fastest post I can.

One last thing. I loved reading your personal notes on your last adventure, but I must warn you that when we submit these for peer review, some publications might be very strict about what they do or do not accept, which may lead to some uncomfortable revisions later on. It might do you rhetorical good to initially leave out the more intrapersonal details in your scientific notes and just include as many ideas and observations from your journey as you can in the actual manuscript. I know these artistic ideas are important to you, so I would accompany this with the recommendation of starting a travel journal, separate from your publication.

Of course, I, as your friend, would love to read those notes as well, but a sort of unforgiving division is necessary for our more empirical audiences.

Write me back soon, James. It was good to hear from you.

— M

3. The Orphan Orchid (*Tacca chantrifolia*)

Location:

Tacca chantrifolia has only been known to naturally grow in the Fujian region of southeast China. While there are as many as ten *Tacca* variations, the striped orphan version is, as far as modern exploration has discovered, endemic to this area. It should be noted that botanical research of the plant is slim, and it is more than likely that the plant could be found throughout the entirety of eastern China and its surrounding islands as opposed to just the Fujian region. The *T. chantrifolia* usually grows in waterlogged, poorly drained areas of the country's rainforests, often in muddy or clay-ridden wetlands or montane drainage ponds. It has never been observed to grow in dry soil. The plant has incredibly low resistance to cold and dies very easily when exposed to temperatures below 55 degrees Fahrenheit (13 degrees Celsius). The opposite is also true; exposure to direct sunlight often leads to a failed cultivation. Because of this, *Tacca chantrifolia* is almost always found in shady patches of undergrowth.

Cultivation:

Before this year, only two attempts to cultivate the plant by itself have been documented. Both of these were in tropical-climate greenhouses, one at the University of Buenos Aires and the other at Westbrook College in Massachusetts. Both failed. Records show that the plant grows well for almost two weeks, but when cultivated alone, it soon develops a yellow coloring around its roots and dies shortly after. The reason for this is still unknown, though it is thought to be caused by insufficient nutrients (suggestions vary between potassium, iron, boron, copper, and even sugar). Due to the rarity of the plant, only a small number of various nutrient surpluses have been studied, and none have successfully led to prolonged solitary cultivation. Another confounding variable is pot size. While nutrient levels are easiest to control in a potted setting, the plant grows at an incredible rate, up to about thirty centimeters. This necessitates multiple repottings per year, each with its own difficulties.

One successful artificial growth does currently exist, but has only been achieved through a grafted cultivation. Recent strides by the Laurey Institute have led to a rather famous bloom of the flower achieved by grafting a severed stalk onto the branch of a waxleaf hedge. Not only did the specimen not die, it thrived in climates far drier than its normal observed habitat. In fact, the experiment was so successful that the particular bloom has since been grafted ten more times to various plants not endemic to the Fujian region. This odd adaptability to grafting has given the flower its prominent public nickname, and ongoing research continues to impress and baffle botanists to this day.

Description:

Similar to its biological cousin, the black orchid or *Tacca chantrieri*, *T. chantrifolia* has one of the darkest pigment makeups of any flowering plant. While perfect blacks are chlorophyllically impossible in nature, the dark violets of the *T. chantrieri* and *T. chantrifolia* both contain the lowest recorded albedo of any naturally occurring botanical pigment (specimens have generated petals ranging in albedo value of 0.2–0.3). *T. chantrifolia*, which is significantly harder to find than its solid black counterpart, also manifests white stripes that originate from each of its clustered flower heads and descend all the way down the whiskers of the plant. This pigmentation was previously thought to be botanically impossible, but, upon discovery, has been substantiated. Though it is commonly mistaken as part of the Orchidaceae family, the *Tacca chantrifolia* is not an orchid, but instead belongs to the same family as the American batflower, yams, and one type of arrowroot.

The plant grows its central flower out of a collection of large bright-green leaves, each measuring over a foot in length. The central stalk, which can contain three to five flowers, measures from 0.6 to 1.1 meters tall. Above the flower grow two large bloom-like leaves called bracts that are the same dark color as the bloom. The flower itself forms as a small bouquet of upward (closed) heads or descended (bloomed) heads that, when open, show a central anther with five surrounding petals. The most striking feature of the flower outside of its bracken wings are its long, filament-like whiskers (bracteoles) that can grow as long as the plant is tall.

Personal Notes:

I arrived in the Port of Xiamen shortly after the end of my last expedition, this time alone. While I did harbor a slight anxiety at the absence of interpreters and guides, in all honesty, I did not feel like I absolutely needed either of them. The orphan orchid, while incredibly rare, bloomed many times in a year, and my experience with the first adventure gave me a rapturous amount of confidence in my newfound abilities. I will not pretend I am incredibly connected to other botanists in my field, few as there are, but after propositioning Marco for this task, he sent some letters, generously translated for me, and was able to acquire the location of a small grove of orphan orchids. The exact methods which he employed to accomplish such a feat I will leave to the reader's imagination, just as they were left to mine. Regardless, after a couple months in the port district, I picked up a small package of supplies (sent ahead by Marco) from the port master and was on my way.

**Letter addressed to James Torrey from Marco Arwaldt
(Delivered with accompanying package)
Port of Xiamen, China
April 10, 1831**

A short note, James.

These supplies are minimal. They should last you only about a week in the wild. I wish I were able to provide you with a guide, but I'm afraid you will have to make do with the map and instructions in this package. I apologize, but it is all I can muster. The Asian Peninsula is a complicated place, but I have faith in your autonomy. Make sure to follow the map as close as you can, and keep an eye out for dangerous animals, difficult terrain, or inclement weather. You will need to buy a horse in the nearby town outside of port, but it is my understanding that the people there are used to such transactions and deal well with Americans.

Good luck, James.

— MA

*

Once I checked out of my lodgings in China, I gained access to a wonderful chestnut horse and saddle. The merchant, a small, hunched-over man, conversed with me shortly in English. He seemed kind and offered me the horse for much less than what I had expected to pay for one, saddle and all. After we shook hands on our deal, he asked me where I was going.

I realized then that I had no good response to this, as I did not know my destination by name. In place of an answer, I pulled out my map and showed the man where my quarry was marked with my finger. His eyes widened a little when he looked at it, and without seeming to think much, he shot a glance up over the mainland behind him.

This concerned me, and I was about to ask him what was wrong, but before I could he looked back at me, smiled a large, enthusiastic smile, and said, "Have a good trip, sir," before shoving the map and scribbled receipt back into my hands and turning away toward his stable. This did nothing to assuage my concerns, but I could do little other than turn away and tug my horse's reins behind me.

The foreboding feeling that I was missing something did not leave as moved westward through the crowded streets. As I walked, I glanced up again and again at the sky, wondering what the man could have been looking at. There was nothing out of the ordinary that I could see. Nothing, not even a single cloud, streaked the perfect pale marble color of the horizon. I stopped looking when my eyes caught the gaze of my new horse, who had been starting and stopping his trot patiently behind me as I slowly progressed through the crowd of people.

He was a beautiful steed, opal white with a powdering of black dust on his flanks and face. His mane and tail were dark and chalky, and he looked incredibly well fed and cared for.

The animal's pensive gaze calmed my anxieties and gave me a sense of security. My ride, at least, was secured, and my journey was planned out by Marco. I needed to simply trust in his ability. The last trip had gone wonderfully. What was I so worried about?

*

At points, I could catch glimpses of a different pale horse in front of me. The random ride of a commuter in the city, to be sure, but the steed that I could barely see through the throng of people and horses crossing between us reminded me of Anisa's horse.

Hers had ducked and dodged between branches and ferns in Sumatra just as my inconsequential leader did through that forest of people.

Fujian itself, on the other hand, was so radically different from Sumatra that I could not stop craning my head at the jutting, teeth-like mountains. The East Indies had been mountainous, but the peaks there were soft, rolling, and connected. Southern China's peaks, on the other hand, took the form of immense rocks protruding from the swampy ground at almost perfect right angles.

From below, they looked like a god had dropped a handful of sharp boulders and left them there, sticking straight out of the muddy ground. The hot air, which had mostly been calm, would sometimes shriek past you like the breath of a giant, and the rocky fence of surrounding mountains made one feel like they were in the process of being eaten by the landscape.

As different as these two regions were, they were equally green. Moss seemed to seep out of every rock, crevasse, and ditch. Tall ferns and shiny tropical leaves covered every inch of land not already swamped by water. The only semblance of civilization past the wooden scaffolding of the port town were the perfectly square rice fields feebly cut out of an ever-encroaching natural progeny.

The grove chosen by Marco was a two-day ride from the port, and I set out into the winding, waterlogged roads immediately after buying my horse. The heat was oppressive, but bearable, and because I remembered to stop frequently to let my horse drink from the many shallow pools of the countryside, we traveled very quickly for the first few hours. In the dull light of the simmering afternoon it even started to rain a warm, invisible drizzle that seemed to materialize out of the humid air in front of my face. Small droplets of condensation clung to the tip of my nose and the metal pieces of my horse's reins.

After one particularly difficult river crossing, I noticed a vivid splotch of color on my left just outside my field of vision. I jerked back on the leather, stopping the horse from the pure shock of it, and discovered that the thing that had caught my eye was a bright, buttery yellow flower. The bloom was a large specimen of the *Chrysanthemum* genus.

This was surprising, as I didn't know at the time that chrysanthemums grew in China. I don't know exactly what it was about the flower, but it also triggered a flood of memories as I stared. Without taking my eyes off of it, I dismounted and knelt down in the mud. The closer I got, the more the memories leapt out, and I was rushed rapidly back to times in my childhood where my mother's chrysanthemums would splay out in the walkway to our front door. The incessant tapping of the rain falling around me calcified my nostalgia for the abrupt and warm western storms. The thin, upcurving petals plucked rain from the air and slowly trickled the water down to the center of the flower. Chrysanthemums had always looked best in the rain.

*

Partially recovered entry from
James Torrey's journal
(Complete document unrecoverable due to damage)
Dated May 30, 1831

It was midsummer, and Amy and I were running down the long road toward my house. In one hand, I clutched a bright yellow daffodil that I had snatched up after school. I had noticed it the day before, but just remembered it that afternoon and decided to take it as a gift to my mother.

It was raining hard, and neither of us had brought a coat of any kind. It had been incredibly sunny that morning, and we were caught off-guard by the flash summer storm. Luckily, the rain was rather warm, but this didn't stop the downpour from soaking through my shirtsleeves and Amy's amber summer dress. Marco would have been with us, but he had needed to go to an eye doctor that day and missed the entire second half of school.

As we rounded the last bend of the fence, I dashed onto the porch, which was protected by the extended roof of the house. Amy hopped up the stairs beside me, pushing her sodden blonde hair to the side, out of her eyes. I found myself staring out at the rain for a second, distracted by the tune of the rapid beat of raindrops splattering out in front of me. The gutter ended just to my left and was overflowing; a cascade of leafy water crackled next to us, boring a hole in the muddy sod at the corner of the stairs. Amy stopped next to me, also looking back at the road.

"Well, let's go inside," I said after a silent minute, turning away from the downpour. My shoes squelched on the dry wooden boards. I opened the door and stepped onto the shoe rug inside.

I had taken off my shoes and even wiped off the water clinging to my bare arms with one of my sweaters before I realized Amy hadn't followed me in. I blinked in surprise, looking back out the door where she was standing, her hands held behind her back.

"Sorry, Jamie, I have to go home now. Better go see how my brother's doing. The rain always gets into that space in between the walls and chills his room. Wish your mother well for me."

She turned quickly and started to walk back into the rain.

"Wait," I said.

The word had jumped out of my mouth without my permission. She turned back and looked in my direction with a curious expression on her face.

I was not sure why I said that. The request had surprised me as much as it had surprised her, but I remember very vividly that, at that moment, the overwhelming urge to give Amy the daffodil washed over me. My arm even extended halfway out as a subconscious reaction, but my muscles caught and froze, arrested by the remembrance of my original intention. This was for my mother, I thought again. That was why I had brought it all this way through the rain, covering it with my soaking wet hand. Even before picking it I had imagined it sitting on the counter the whole run home, its buttery hue coloring the atmosphere of the kitchen.

I found myself staring dumbly, first at the flower, and then back at Amy. It must have been the color of her dress that had made me think of changing my mind. It matched the cupped yellow petals of the plant as if they had been cut from the same cloth.

"What's the matter?" she asked, just slightly tilting her head to the left.

"N—Nothing," I replied, bringing my arm back in and turning around. "Give my best wishes to your brother for me."

I awkwardly walked a little farther into the house without looking back, then realized I had forgotten to close the door. I turned around again.

Amy was already out of view. The doorway lay empty, and the patter of rain continued to beat out its rhythm on the roof.

*

I pushed all the way until nightfall, which I realized retroactively was an incredible lapse in judgment. I still hadn't made a fire or cooked any food by the time the sun set behind the mountains and doing so in the dark proved almost impossible. In the end, I decided to use the small amount of lamp oil I had brought to start a fire, and then used the fire for both light and cooking. I reminisced piningly about how luxurious it had been to have a companion whose sole purpose was to provide light for the party just a few months in the past.

Even with the oil's sacrifice giving me the gift of light and a drying heat, my night was a miserable one. I had not anticipated how utterly damp and rainy the trip would be, and I awoke the next morning shivering in the dew. As I prepared to leave, another pang of frustration hit me when I realized that my entire cotton bag and leather saddle had soaked through with the rolling fog of the morning. My food had survived, but the start of that day was one of the most drudgingly difficult undertakings I can remember. The warm breeze, which I thought would dry out my equipment, was counteracted by the vicious humidity of the lowland air. Crossing streams, though no water touched me, completely undid any drying effect of the rising sun, which was a vacuous reflection of the sunrise I had with Anisa in the Sumatran wilderness.

With this misery came the inability to travel for very long, and I made frequent stops to let my horse drink and to rotate the clothes I hung from my pack in a feeble attempt to expose them to the sunlight. By midafternoon, I was exhausted, and so was my horse. I could feel blisters forming on the sides of my toes and the bottoms of my heels. The metal stirrups and my soaked socks had only exacerbated this inevitable process.

As I adjusted my damp map for the last time and slowly tempted my horse to walk through a thick bushel of sawgrass, we stumbled awkwardly into the clearing Marco had marked on my map. It was so strange; the feat which had seemed so momentous in Sumatra now seemed almost sad, like the whimper of a mine worker as he falls onto his bed after a grueling day's work. I was so tired that I rolled my mat onto the ground and fell asleep before even attempting to look for the orphan orchid.

I awoke the next morning slightly revitalized and excited to finally take down the dimensions and characteristics of the flower. Though I had seen bat orchids before, their estranged, white-striped cousin was an anomaly, and I was anxious to be one of the few scientists in the world to witness the plant in a natural setting. The prospect did not completely push away the encroaching doubt that had accumulated like dust in my brain from the grueling journey, but it lightened my mental load enough for me to drag myself off of my bedroll and shake the dew out of my hair.

*

The search was initially difficult and unfruitful. After almost an hour of looking, I was considering the horrible possibility that my information was fallacious, and that no flowers were here except the common water lotus and some Chinese lilies. My mind fluttered with thoughts of Marco's letters being sent, translated, decoded, answered, decoded again, and retranslated, bringing up visions of the old "whispers" game we would play as children in primary school. But finally, after circling the pond at the center of the clearing three times, out of the corner of my eye I spotted the broad spade-like leaves of the *Tacca* genus and traced them around the curve of the pond until I saw my first flash of stygian stripes.

The flower looked more like the traditional Asian design of a dragon than that of a bat. Its whiskers, much longer and thicker than I had expected, hung around the descended flower buds like the jowls of an animal. The flower was miraculously alone, allegedly an oddity for the species. Yet there it stood, tall and slender next to the encroaching grass. The two uplifted bracken wings hovered magically on top of the zebra-shaded petals, protecting its slight form from the drizzling rain that had started up again. I stared at it for a while, and then eagerly waded back through the grass and ferns toward my horse and camp. Reaching into my bag, I fumbled around looking for my pad and pencil in order to note the flower's dimensions and special characteristics.

Finally, my fingers grasped the binding and yanked it free.

With a sinking feeling that soon turned into a plummet, I noticed that the whole thing, having been unceremoniously stuffed to the bottom of the bag, was as soaked through as my saddle. The pressed white parchment was stuck together in one brick of waterlogged tissue, ruined beyond repair.

Admitting this into a book of plants is dramatic and unprofessional, but it must be said. I cannot instill upon you, the reader, how far this sank what was left of my spirit. The recollection of the plant's description has been done from memory only, and some of the figures are estimates at best, but my trip was thoroughly ruined in that moment. I simply slumped to the side of my pack and cried like a child, completely overtaken by my failure. A pitiful sight, really. A grown man, crying next to his horse because his notebook got wet.

But it was more than that. I had come so far . . . alone for the first time. In that moment, so removed from help and friendly faces, I had only myself to rely on in that damp jungle, and, deprived of the sole immediate duty to record, I felt so alone. I had no Anisa to laugh at my ridiculous profession. No mother to shoo me into a hot bath at home, and no Marco to tell me what not to forget.

I sat there, just staring at the dripping grove before me for what must have been over an hour, the rain mixing with the salty stains of my drying tears. After getting up and walking back over to the flower, I just stood there, looking at it. Eventually my gaze slowly wandered from the solitary plant and drifted again and again over the lake and into the sky. The clouds were omnipresent that day, covering the entirety of the horizon in a solid, featureless gray.

After a few hours in the clearing, I stood up from my reverie, resolved to leave.

But, at the moment of exodus, I was gripped with an unshakeable feeling of angst. My frustration shifted into a twinge of what almost felt like anger. I felt cheated, unfairly treated by the journey and the day. So, before leaving the clearing, I did something I had never done before and will hopefully never do again.

I picked the flower.

Perhaps the knowledge that the plant could be grafted was what allowed this idea to take hold of me. Perhaps not. But I did do it. Walking briskly back to the spot I had left, I plucked its round, vibrant stem from the ground, tearing it off just below its lowest leaf. It released easily, snapping like the corded striations of a stick of celery.

As I walked back over to my pack, reality began to drip back into my brain. I knew grafting was a careful process. There was simply no physical way for me to successfully keep the plant alive long enough to graft anyway, despite its unusual qualities.

I reached my horse and saddle, still holding the dying flower in my hand as I flipped open my saddle packs and pulled the sodden notebook out again. Opening its sopping wet pages, I placed the slain dragon in between them.

However, like a seesaw, I again descended back toward humiliating embarrassment. My anger morphed back into a sodden regret, and before I could shut the pages, I took the flower back out and laid it on the steaming ground.

*

After that, I left, soaked to the heart and the core, pushing my horse through the same pile of sawgrass I had stumbled over the evening before. I dreaded the final night, not wanting to sleep again in the damp chill of the rainforest, but I consoled myself by waking early with the diffuse red sunlight and finishing, at least superficially, the last leg of my journey. I didn't even stay a night in Xiamen, but boarded the anchored shipping vessel without a word to another person besides the harbormaster. My door was unlocked, and I spent the night huddled in my cot, dressed in the driest clothes I had, listening to the slop of the sea against the ship's wooden hull. Sometime during the night, rain started to patter over the deck, sending thin strips of water down the outside of my room's porthole.

Letter addressed to Marco Arwaldt from Daniel Heath

Royal Botanical Publishing

Gloucester, UK

June 29, 1831

Dear Marco,

My boy! It has been too long. Why, it seemed like only yesterday you were here in Britain with me having breakfast near the Thames. It is good to hear from you again. You absolutely must visit this next semester; I have a business class that is in need of a competent assistant. We have also just published our newest addition to the botanical library, "Arthur's Botany," and it has gotten great reviews by top experts in the field. I have no doubt that the university would not mind introducing you to Arthur McAlister himself, if that is something you or your acquaintances desire.

With all that being said, I do intend to give you feedback on the partial manuscript you sent to us the other month. I must admit that I was surprised, Marco. This text is far different from anything you have vouched for before. Why, just last year I remember we published a manuscript you were an agent for on botanical pedagogy and its alternative benefits. Now _that_ was a masterpiece. The writing was fine, but the construction of the piece, from my understanding at least, greatly changed how the professors here at the university looked at didactic botany and scientific literature. I truly cannot praise it enough.

This new manuscript, however . . . well, I must just admit that a shred of disappointment has lodged in between my brain and my skull, if you catch my drift. The writing is more poetic than pedagogical, and much of the article's length does not deal with the subject matter at all. I might be able to convince the publishing council to accept a shortened version with vast sections cut out, but I would not be a very good friend if I didn't tell you about my apprehensions when it comes to peer review. The council I can influence, but peers in the field . . .

No, with this current manuscript, I must sadly reject a contract at this time. Though do not think that your reputation is damaged in this interaction. I still have faith in your work, and you have proven more than capable of finding and recommending incredible work for the university journal. If you cut out some of the unnecessary narrative in the middle of the work, I'm sure we can come to an agreement in the future.

Please understand. If it were up to me, I would accept it with changes, but I just can't convince my superiors that this is the best we can do. My mailbox is always open, and I look forward to receiving more manuscripts in the future that better align with the council's vision for the journal.

Yours, Daniel Heath

Letter addressed to James Torrey from Marco Arwaldt
Black Hawk, TN, USA
August 25, 1831

Dear James,

I have just read your letter. You have my apologies. I cannot shake the feeling that, if I had supplied you with better rations and gear, this could have been avoided. Again, I'm truly sorry.

As for your draft and what you sent of your journal notes, I have received them. I'm sure you are very anxious, but do not worry; I have used a little bit of my free time to do some more research into the subject of past explorations and found a few relevant testimonials on the orphan orchid that we neglected before. We can insert some information from them into the previous section in place of your lost notes, I'm sure.

Unfortunately, I do have some more bad news. I submitted your primary manuscript from your first expedition to my good friend Dr. Heath at the Royal Botanical Institute. He is a very kind man, and a good friend from my early days in England. While he praised the effort of your undertaking, he informed me that the Institute's publishing company would not be able to commit to a publication as is. I know this is hard, and I must confess I had misgivings about piling this information on you so soon after such a difficult journey. I am sorry, but you must not lose your spirit. Our plans are good ones, James, and this is something you have wanted to do for a long time. You won't be beaten . . . I know it.

In that vein, I have a couple helpful suggestions. Firstly, that the focus of the future pieces could, perhaps, be concentrated even further on the pure data of the plants. This is something Dr. Heath suggested, and while I agree, I also promise you that much of that can be left to me in the editing phase. It was wonderful to hear about your interactions with Anisa and the sailors, but do not feel too downtrodden if such passages might be stricken from the edited manuscript. They are beautiful writings, and we will keep what we can, but a honed silver scalpel is often more appealing to these publishers than the warm wooden mallet.

Secondly, I believe that we should move up your expedition in search of the S. estrellas to make it your next quarry.

This will give you some breathing room, as it is in America, and will, I believe, ease the burden of your recent travels. Please let me know if those suggestions are agreeable to you, and I will make the proper arrangements. As always, I look forward to your letters.

— M

4. The Stylite Star (*Solus estrellas*)

Location:

Solus estrellas, while not indigenous to the States, is now isolated to the western plains of North America and usually found in the open fields of the frontier just east of the Mississippi River. Records of its locational origin vary widely, and a definite starting point of natural growth is difficult to discern. However, it is known that its introduction to the United States was most likely accomplished by accident through new eastern trade routes from either Africa or Asia.

It should be noted that *S. estrellas*'s namesake characteristic is its habit to only grow in solitary conditions. Out of the dozen or so recorded sightings of the plant, no buds have been witnessed to grow less than six kilometers apart. This abnormal and rather curious phenotypical characteristic makes the flower incredibly difficult to find and has greatly contributed to its reputation as an invisible species, despite actual global population estimates ranging in the hundreds. The plant usually grows on high, grassy plains, surviving best in well-drained soil. It has also purportedly shown an incredible ability to survive in nutrient-deprived soil, which is quite common throughout the American prairies. This fact, however, has been difficult to substantiate in artificial cultivations. *S. estrellas* has also been reported to grow well with the *Hesperostipa comata* grass species. The grass is unfortunately much taller than the *S. estrellas*, making this neighborly relationship ironically detrimental to the flower's discovery and study in the wild.

Cultivation:

Cultivation of the *S. estrellas*, unlike that of many other species in this study, is relatively straightforward. The species has orthodox methods of germination, growth, flowering, and pollination and can therefore be grown easily in most modern botanical gardens. However, due to its members' inability to grow in proximity coupled with their inability to self-pollinate, it is necessary to cultivate two to three plants in different pots. Strangely, the plant has also been shown to fail in the flowering stage if grown too close to other plants of its kind, despite being planted and cultivated in different fixtures. Therefore, an appropriately large greenhouse (or one with adequate physical separation between cultivations) is also needed for proper care of multiple specimens (a distance of three hundred meters or a refined division of the plants has proven to be sufficient). Though cultivation is superlatively simple, domestic use is almost nonexistent due to the rarity of the seeds and disproportionate amount of effort it takes to care for the plant versus its small amount of decorative yield.

Description:

Similar to the much more common starflower, the efflorescence of the *Solus estrellas*, or stylite star as it is commonly called, manifests as a single small bloom (three to five centimeters in diameter) with simple, ocular petals that grow in whorls of six at the end of a very thin stem (1.2 centimeters in circumference at the most). The flower, which is also commonly called the stylite star, has no leaves or secondary growths, making it exceedingly difficult to identify in the wild. Its central stamens are unusually large and extend out from the face of the flower for one to two centimeters. The petals range from a buttery yellow to a mellow orange, unlike their snow-white counterparts (*Solus blancus*). The *S. blancus* also grows primarily in the prairie regions of the central United States but lacks the *S. estrellas*'s solitary growing habits.

The *S. estrellas* grows from a thin, creeping rhizome and blooms for up to four weeks a year. In controlled cultivations, this always occurs near the tail end of the fall season, and the blooms mature rapidly under moderate to intense sunlight.

Personal Notes:

This trip, which I had originally planned to take on last, was moved forward for travel purposes. Marco deemed it requisite and necessary for me to stay in America—less than six hundred miles west from my hometown, even. I agreed.

I arrived at a small inn-house on the bank of the Mississippi near the end of November.

"A poorly chosen date," I was told by the master of the house, as the untamed West usually had heaps of snow at this point. However, through some remarkable manifestation of luck, I spent the first two weeks of my trip in as good a weather as I could have hoped. While my hosts were an old, frail couple who looked like they had been on the river for one too many winters, it was lovely to have company again after my purgatory of loneliness on the other side of the Atlantic.

The enumerator of my poor plannings, an old ashen man by the name of Charles Earp, would sit at the fire in the small living room and read various papers that he had lying everywhere. I was told by his wife, a cautious woman of some sixty or so years, that he had been an excellent engineer in his youth and had built many bridges across the wide Mississippi. These bridges were apparently the subjects of the various papers he obsessively pored over every night, straining his eyes to read the scribbled text that he had probably written decades before.

What he could want with the strewn, disorganized plans of completed projects, I could not hope to imagine. Nonetheless, having a silent companion to sit with by the fire every night brought a profound comfort to me and renewed my zeal for my own passion. I could almost envision myself, forty or so years in the future, poring over heaps upon heaps of notes about the flora of the world in my own small living room. This escape into the future rekindled a wonderful sense of contentment and purpose. *Perhaps I would even be able to accommodate some young, annoying adventurers in their pursuits,* I thought. And like that, my thoughts tumbled back on themselves in pleasant revolutions for entire evenings.

I had always thought the West was much the same as Tennessee, but this is not so. Where Tennessee had miles and miles of flat, monochrome farmland, the West was eerily untamed. Its hills rolled almost imperceptibly over each other. The horizon was deeper and lent itself to beautifully broad and vivid sunsets.

There were two piles of hay stacked at least six meters tall next to the house, and I was easily able to climb them like a playful boy and watch as the hills gently cradled the sun until it slept. In my previous journeys, I had been awed by the incredible infinitude of the sea's horizon, under the impression that the magnitude of that skyline was unmatched—but the brilliant vista of the unmapped steppes was equally, if not more, enveloping.

The Mississippi River was its own monster as well. Though I had been an adventurous child, I had never traveled to the frontier before this trip. The river was enormous. It might seem strange for a man who has seen the sea, the waterfalls of Sumatra, and the towering, rocky teeth of China to be impressed by an American river, but it instilled in me a kind of insufficiency, an overpowering sense of smallness, that I have never felt before or since.

It carried a black, undulating, and ever-moving current, so unlike the waves of the ocean, that shocked me with its speed and darkness. The low rumble of waves cascading against the tall, sheer banks echoed back and forth over the expanse. Being stationed in its northernmost section, I was not even at its widest part, a carnally mystifying concept that proved hard for me to grasp. Even if this book never gets published, and my dream of botanical ingenuity is never realized, I will always be grateful to this trip for showing me just how large nature can be.

*

In the evening near the tail end of my two weeks of preparation, I was stuffing a hiking backpack in front of the fire —making sure not to disturb the piles of precariously stacked papers on the adjacent desks, coffee tables, and hearth— when I heard a knock at the door. I say a knock, but it was more of a belligerent banging. The door's assailant pounded mightily on the knocker three or four times in a row, paused for a few seconds, resumed, and then repeated that cycle again and again.

 Malinda, the wife of the obsessive engineer, regarded the door nervously from her vantage point at the top of the stairwell. Slowly, she walked down the stairs and looked through a small crack in the wall paneling to see who it was.

"It's her," she whispered harshly in Mr. Earp's direction. The man grunted beside me in apparent response. The old woman bit her lip before turning back to the door, unlocking it and letting it swing open.

With a massive thud, a huge form fell through the doorway and landed on the hardwood floor. A person, who had apparently leaned this cargo on the locked door while they announced their arrival, now stepped over the dropped mass.

"Just leave it on the floor," said the wife in a tone that to me sounded a little cold.

A pair of black leather boots were the only objects I could see in front of the shining backdrop of the setting sun, and I blinked dumbly as the figure proceeded to pull the heavy load inside, out of the cold western wind.

It was thirty seconds before I realized that the huge bulk was a dead deer, and a minute more before the door was finally closed and I noticed that the bearer of the beast looked familiar. As they lifted their head, the brim of their hat slowly tipped up, revealing a shining, if not slightly scratched-up face. Short, loose curls fell into view . . . a sharp chin . . . a pair of steely eyes. And then the full face was revealed. The person in the doorway, to my bewilderment, was none other than Amy Willers.

She had changed about as much as a person could change in a decade and a half. Gone were the linen dresses she had worn to school. Instead, she wore a farmer's leather short-jacket, loose-fitting twill cowboy pants pulled over the heavy looking boots, and a white cotton shirt, the collar of which was bent and smudged with dirt from carrying the deer. Her head was mostly covered by the wide hat that had shadowed her eyes when she burst in. But now that I could see her in the red light of the stove fire, I recognized the rounded cheek bones, the high forehead, and the light-colored pupils. She looked strong, and very much like she was no longer scared of crab spiders.

"Amy?" I managed to choke out. She leveled her gaze at my hapless, crouched form, hunched over a canvas backpack and surrounded by piles of papers. Her eyes widened in realization and surprise.

"Well, I'll be damned. Is that Jamie Torrey?"

I unrooted myself and stood from my task. Slowly, I walked toward her, knocking over a paper stack without realizing it. My mind was racing with surprise and excitement. My mouth opened and closed wordlessly. By the time I got to her, I was still unsure whether I should give her a hug or a handshake.

*

We talked all through the night, sitting with cups of tea next to the warm fire. At dusk, Mr. Earp grunted disapprovingly, got up, and left his chair a full two hours earlier than usual, no doubt annoyed by our rather rude and rambunctious disruption of what had previously been a peacefully silent study.

After leaving Tennessee at fourteen, Amy had apparently quit school altogether. I remembered her mentioning something back then before she left, but I had already been told I was to leave for secondary school in Deadwood, a town almost fifty miles away, and at the time was more worried about my fate than anyone else's.

"You forgot about me, Jamie! How rude, really." She made sure to accompany this remark with a smile. "I imagine Deadwood wasn't really that exciting, was it?"

She was right. My time in secondary had been incredibly boring and almost stifled my will to pursue higher education. The classes were generally dull, and most depressingly, the town was almost entirely devoid of gardens.

Shortly after my departure, she had left with her family to live in the warmer South, near Georgia. They intended to care for her sick brother together. Apparently, they had an aunt who owned a small medical business in the area and thought that the coastal air would do him some good. Unfortunately, the plan was of no avail, and he died almost a year later. In the wake of his death, the family had almost no one to undertake the laborious work of maintaining the farm that they had bought when they moved, so the responsibility fell to Amy.

"You can't wear a dress while driving a plow," she told me that night, and the additional changes to her appearance all followed that same limiting factor. Long hair got caught easily. Decorative hats protected the skin little from the sun's daily assault. Cotton shirts were easy to clean and even easier to replace. She had worked the life of a farmhand for almost seven years, tending to everything that her aging father couldn't, and was the saving grace of her family (though not the most ladylike one).

"It didn't really matter—what someone wore, I mean," she said. "We all went to the barn dances just the same."

Though they had been able to scrape out a living in Georgia, she finally convinced them to move back out west—away from the deathplace of her poor brother—and to settle down with a cousin who owned another farm near the Mississippi. This unfortunately proved to be another bad decision, as the cousin had lied to Amy about the stability of his farm. Before the next three years were up, the farm had to be sold, and the crushing weight of responsibility fell, again, to her. On top of that, her mother died of an unknown illness only a year later. It was said around town that she had never fully recovered from her son's death. Afterward, Amy sold what was left of the farm and returned to the West to look for work. I realized she hadn't mentioned where her father was, and I didn't have the courage to ask.

Evidently, Amy's kindness had not come to the same fate as her long hair, and no disdain or malice was evident in her voice when I related the past decade of my schooling to her. There was only a careful interest in the happenings of my life and occasional interjections of questions regarding Marco and other friends from back home. I felt rather uncomfortable during this conversation. She spoke to me as if nothing had changed, as if nothing were different between her and me—me, who had been lucky enough to go to a university and study flowers, of all things.

The deer (which had been unceremoniously left to sit on the hardwood floor by Amy and Mrs. Earp for the initial part of our conversation, but by now had been silently dragged away by the latter) was part of a few favors she performed for the household. I learned with more surprise that the raw meat that provided the basis for the meals I had been eating for the last two weeks had been primarily supplied by Amy herself. Hunting, it turns out, came easy to her, and she quite enjoyed roaming the many large woodland valleys of the prairie and presenting her spoils to her family and friends. The trade also came with its benefits, one of which was paying back accrued debts. With zeal, she showed me the bullet wound firmly placed under the left shoulder of the poor animal.

"A perfect shot," she remarked with a grin of pride.

Before we knew it, our tea was cold, and the moon had already completed its westward journey over the plains to make room for the coming sun. It was only then, under the influence of sleepiness and the exhilarating drunkenness of talking to a friend, that I mustered the courage to ask her if she wanted to accompany me on my quest for the stylite star.

At first, she laughed awkwardly in response. Then, after a moment of silence, she got up from her chair and put her coat on without saying anything or looking at me.

"I'm serious!" I continued, getting up too. "It wont take more than a week with the two of us."

We stood there for a second. She looked like she was contemplating something over my left shoulder. She sat deep in thought for what must have been a full minute. Finally, with a sigh, she refocused her eyes on my face and regarded my awkward form with half-closed lids, the ending of a contemplative purse still staining her mouth.

"Have you ever forded a river as big as the Mississippi, Jamie?"

I was taken aback. Embarrassment started to creep back into my brain. After a few seconds of silence, she laughed again and turned toward the door, waving her hand over her head.

"I'll help you find your flower, although first I have some business to attend to. I'll be back in two days." She opened the door and stood there in the darkness, silhouetted by the sable glow of the dawning sky. "A week, huh? You sure that's what it'll take?"

"A week." I answered.

Her head bobbed down in a nod, her hat widening out the silhouette of her face into an oblong oval. "Good morning, James," she said, and then the door closed silently behind her.

*

Finally, in that dark early morning, I walked up the stairs and across the hall toward my small, rented room. I tread carefully over the creaky boards of the upper floor, trying to make as little sound as possible. My mind swam with excitement at the coming trip, but the weariness from the sleepless night had returned as soon as Amy had left. I opened the door in silence, curved my body around it and swung it back inward. Just as I was about to close it completely, however, I thought I saw the glint of eyes in the darkness. I paused, the door half shut, and looked again into the deep shadow of the hall. Across from my room at the other end of the corridor lay the Earps' room, and it had appeared for a moment that the door was slightly ajar. The brief flashes of light I thought were eyes had seemed to come from that direction, but as I looked again, I saw that the small breach of shadow in the doorway had disappeared, and the door lay solid and closed above the darkened stairwell.

*

A two-day waiting period was perfect, and by the time Amy came trotting up the long road south of the country house, I was there to meet her on my newly acquired horse, bundled up against the mild wind and laden with only the essentials. I had been very meticulous when selecting my gear this time, not only to prepare for the possibility of rain, which had made my last trip such a horrible undertaking, but also to impress Amy with my self-sufficiency. Of course, her pleasant demeanor did not show any truly ardent signs that she thought little of me, but I still felt an eagerness to please her with my preparation and readiness.

"Ready? Let's be off!" she said into the wind, and off we went, following the chasmic curves of the great river. The hills where there was the greatest chance of finding the flower were fifty-three miles north of the inn, about a two-day journey. The hours flew by this time, in contrast to my seemingly infinite slog through the swamps of China for the *T. chantrifolia*. Having Amy along was a drug all on its own, and we talked throughout the entire trip, barely taking breaks to eat. She had always been an excellent talker. Instead of prattling on and on about her own grievances, she would ask interesting and sometimes deeply personal questions again and again without a hint of embarrassment.

"What are your parents doing now?"

"Did you miss the country?"

"How boring was school? I couldn't imagine!"

"Do you have *any* friends, now? Well, besides Marco, I mean?"

I appreciated her attention more than I ever had in our younger days and attempted to ask her as many questions as she asked me, struggling all the while. Regardless, the next couple of days were magical in their simplicity. Talking while wandering by horse over the endless hills of the western expanse filled each day with new information about the person she had become, glimpses into her new character. She was lively and excited, something I was deeply surprised by considering the hardships she had so recently endured and the ones she still faced. Debt, it sounded like, was the one thing she refused to talk about. I did not press.

We ate a variety of homemade meals that I had paid Mrs. Earp to prepare, and the warm steam of the fire-toasted muffins brought back memories of Tennessee. It was as if I had leapt back ten years in time.

It was soon clear that I could not have chosen a better guide. After I told her of the flower's growing habits, she quickly disregarded the rudimentary notes I had on possible locations and replaced almost every spot with a new, more auspicious hiding spot. Despite taking me on multiple small excursions to look in sloping rock outcrops and increasingly winding gullies, she always ended the day in a suitable camp location near water and shade. She told me she had camped out on the prairie many times hunting for deer and buffalo, and that she knew this side of the river better than anyone north of Missouri. We shared a tent at night, as it was easier to carry one tent than two, and my horse was already laden down with various maps, food, and botany books. Before, these relics had been a profound comfort to me, but this time I found myself ignoring them altogether.

On the third night, Amy had been talking for almost an hour in our small camp tent about her job as a courier for a town butcher shop (one of the many prestigious titles she had gathered over the years) when she saw me rustling through my papers.

We had a small travel lamp burning just outside the tent whose light blurred as it passed through the thin cloth, illuminating the interior with a warm, shadowless glow, and I had been trying to read some of my personal notes from previous trips in order to remember the name of the ship I took to Sumatra. I noticed Amy looking over my shoulder.

"Why, Jamie, you haven't got any pictures in your book, have you?" she said.

Taken aback, I mumbled that I didn't. The University textbooks had always had some artistic renditions in them, but the thought had never occurred to me that I should include visuals of my planned flowers. The descriptions, I had thought, would be enough to show what the specimens look like, and I related to her this train of thought. Amy's indignation quickly voided me of this idea.

"Here," she said, sitting up quickly from her leather sleeping roll. "Give me one of the descriptions. I know how to draw pretty well from my mother." I complied with her request, giving her a spare draft of the description of my mother's lilacs. She took the draft and one of my pencils, and right then and there started to sketch out the flower on the back side of the notes. I watched her for a while, mesmerized by how she licked her fingers and smudged the pencil marks to make the different shades of the shadows look more realistic.

After a while and without looking up she said, "You better get some sleep. Drawing takes a while."

Quietly, I rolled over to face the wall of the tent still lit by the flickering lantern burning outside and fell asleep to the soft scratching of her drawing pencil on my note paper.

*

Amy, as I had noticed both that night and the night of our unsuspecting rendezvous, had the incredible ability to stay up all night and not lose vivacity. However, I found out the next evening of our trip that this incredible power of determination was not without its repercussions. That night we chose a rather swampy hollow to sleep in, mostly for its access to water, but also because Amy was about to drop out of her saddle. The labor of both today and yesterday's haul combined with a full thirty-six sleepless hours seemed to be the limit of even her preternatural powers. I could tell that she was attempting to keep herself together, but our conversation had grown increasingly and uncharacteristically one-sided. Finally, after rapidly cooking something to eat and devouring it in only a couple bites, she retired to the barely standing tent and passed out on her leather.

I could barely keep myself from laughing at the newfound humanity of my friend that had been brought up from the depths of her powerful atmosphere. Her guard had finally been dropped under the godlike power of exhaustion prolonged two rhythms too long.

After cleaning up the camp, I hung what remained of our food in a tree away from our tent just like the monk had during my pursuit of the corpse flower. I then slipped inside as well and doused the lantern.

I could not sleep that early, it turned out, and I lay looking at my side of the tent for the first two hours of my struggle against the accumulated energy of the day. At first, I thought too much about the flower, the original object of my search. We had not seen anything as we wandered over hill after promising hill, and I was starting to feel that this might be the flower I would be unable to find. Our food and supplies would only last a few more days at most, and my mind reeled at the thought of returning to the engineer's house empty-handed and starving. It would be better, I kept repeating in my head, to be only one of those things.

Still, these problems seemed miniscule compared to the enjoyment of the last week of camping on the plains. The company of a friend was something I had somewhat lost after college, and it was almost as if Amy had dragged me back to my country-style childhood, lilacs and all.

I adjusted myself to feel more comfortable during my nostalgic mental excursion and eventually landed on my back with my hands clasped under my neck, staring at the soft cloth of the sloped tent roof. Amy's previously frozen body shuffled beside me. In one startling motion, she flopped over onto her side, now facing me, and her arm gently came to rest on my bent elbow. She let out a quiet sigh as she did so. As the motion ceased, the tent fell back into its quiet tranquility, with only the chirping of insects and the soft breeze interrupting the quietude.

Almost shocked into shying away, I overcame my initial unconscious reaction. Carefully, I turned my head, lifting it slightly from my entwined fingers in order to look at her face. Her brow was slightly furrowed, giving her powerful features a childish, tired look, but her eyes were still lightly shut. From the soft rise and fall of her chest, I could tell that she was still fast asleep, the steady rhythm of her breathing just as slow and slight as before.

I didn't want to move, embarrassed that we were so close. I thought multiple times about waking her up but couldn't bring myself to disturb her exhausted sleep.

After that, I could no longer think of memories or flowers. I made several more attempts to fall asleep with her hand still on my arm, hoping coyly that she might eventually wake up during my slumber and have a chance to experience this circumstance as I had, but that endeavor soon proved futile. She was out like a light, and I could not extinguish myself.

Eventually, I resolved to move, and inch by inch, tugged my torso to the left, holding my breath like a child trying to sneak out from under the covers. Without a sound, her fingers slowly tipped off my arm and fell to rest on the tent floor. Proceeding carefully, I got up, grabbed my boots from their resting spot right outside the entrance, and shuffled silently out of the tent. After getting my notes from my pack, I sat contentedly on a log near our camp and leafed through them, looking for the drawing Amy had finished the night before. My eyes had adjusted to nightfall, and the moon shone appraisingly through the high clouds.

I eventually found it and sat there for some time staring at the dark lines of the flower. The light of the moon fluctuated as clouds ebbed past, causing the deep pigment blots to swim in and out of focus. The drawing was an incredible rendition of my mother's lilacs. Even devoid of color, I could almost smell them through the page, sending me further and further into my own mental drama. Each puff of flowering blossom was lightly shadowed and placed against a slightly darkened backdrop. They looked as if they floated there, held in space by an imaginary hand. The curves of the petals vortexed into each other: lifelike, pale, and soft, made almost animate with the illusory powers of starlight.

After what must have been ten minutes of staring at Amy's drawing, I started to lay my notebook next to me, but as the pages fell over each other, I noticed that there were more dark marks further along in my notes. I picked it up again and thumbed through it. My eyes widened as I turned past the second entry. There on the page stood an almost perfect replica of the orphan orchid. I flipped even further, and soon realized exactly what had taken her all night to accomplish. She had made renditions of the corpse flower, the orphan orchid, the stylite, and every other plant I had yet to find, save the last. She must have gleaned their appearances from the cursory notes I had taken down from my botany books during my preparations. In the margin of the notes for the absent flower, she had scribbled "Not enough details" and included a small drawn face with an exaggerated frown. I sat staring at them all for a while. They were utterly beautiful. For nearly half an hour I must have stayed there, examining each of them in turn like precious stones.

After a time, I shut the notebook and laid it beside me. The rustling sound of the prairie was alive around me. I looked up and waited for my eyes to adjust to the far-off abyss of the breezy steppe's midnight luster. The blurry movement of the grass came first, followed closely by the outline of dark bracken trees. Out further, near the horizon, the rocks of the endless llanos jutted out like the teeth of an enormous saw. In my imagination, I flew out through the warm air, zipping from peak to peak, looking in every niche for the stylite star. I fleeted from rock to rock, checking in between grass patches, threading through plant stalks, and flashing past tall, wind-blasted prairie trees. But . . . despite flying past every valley, rock outcrop, and prairie hill, I found nothing. My prize eluded my phantasmal form. Even in my imagination it was absent.

I closed my eyes. A gentle patter crept around me.

It started to rain.

With the encroaching mist, my imaginative pneuma returned, speeding in reverse over the far fields and back into myself. My prize was locked away now, I felt it—the path to it blocked by a watery cage with a million descending bars. After a while I opened my eyes to the warm darkness and its rain. Carefully, I pulled the closed notebook under my shirt to keep it dry.

As I got up from the log, a resolution cemented itself inside my mind, and, walking as quietly as I could to the tent, I carried back within me the fully formed intention to ask Amy to accompany me on the remaining expeditions of my quest.

*

We woke the next day earlier than usual. Her hibernation had done its job, and she was as lively and spry as ever. I told her that we should only continue for a couple more days; I explained it was possible that, this time at least, the *S. estrellas* simply had not bloomed, and that we might have to come back next year.

She made no sign that she understood my rather childish hint at a future trip together, and instead furrowed her brow and asked, "Could we not at least look until Sunday, Jamie? I was hoping to show you this marvelous rock out near Spotters' Gulch. It's got as good a spot as ever to find your flower."

As she said so, she rather abruptly pulled out the map she had been using to guide us and hastily pointed to a swampy green mark indicating a lowered arroyo.

I replied that I wasn't sure if we had enough food to continue the trip too much further, and that I had told Mrs. Earp that I would be arriving back on Friday. Accounting for the time it would take to return, that meant we would need to leave after two more days of travel north at most.

"Oh . . .," she replied with a blank expression on her face. "You should have told me that."

The whole conversation was a little more strained than usual, but I shrugged this thought off and continued setting up my horse. I did wish that the trip could be prolonged, and in the short silence that fell between us I came to the conclusion that she might just share that desire as well. This could not be, however. We simply didn't have enough supplies to keep wandering northward up the river. She knew that.

"All right, then," she said in a thin voice after everything was packed away. "Let's be off."

That night, too, swam with these strange silences. Eventually, I forcefully resolved to let go of this feeling, hoping my travel proposal, which I had decided to bring up once we reached the inn, would set things right again.

It was not until well after midday the next day that I truly started to regret focusing on such a ridiculous thing for so long. I had barely taken in the beautiful morning and afternoon of the golden-gray prairie. Strangely, after my mind adjusted to the idea of returning to the house soon, I did not feel sad about the possibility of this being the first time I would miss my quarry. Though I had failed, I had a friend, and the new invigorating feeling of anticipation for a future companionship. These thoughts swam in my head all through the afternoon and into the evening, and seemed to lighten even the footsteps of my horse as we started riding back south. The setting sun was on our right side, its bleeding red beams skipping over the cold waters of the mighty Mississippi. My ember of a question burned at the tip of my tongue the entire rest of that day.

*

We arrived on the long wagon road that approached the house from behind on the morning of the third day heading back. I was trotting slowly in front and Amy's horse followed quietly in the rear. I found myself nervous but happy during the final day of our return journey. My thoughts swam with the wonderful breakfast that Mrs. Earp was preparing for her tired old husband, and I could almost smell the coffee fumes drifting from the dark windows of the house. The thought reminded me of Sumatra, and my mind quickly took delight in the shining similarities. The sunlight, the flowers, the horses, the coffee, a partner—each vividly resurfaced in my memory as the low rush of the river echoed around us.

No lights shone from the inside, signaling a fire had not yet been started, but I was sure that once the presence of visitors was confirmed, it would be whipped up in no time. I prodded my horse up to the porch, dismounted, and tied it off. Amy's horse drew up next to mine and she began to dismount. Then, through the thin morning air, a sharp cry split the silence like shattered glass.

I froze, listening carefully and putting my hand up behind me to stop Amy's steps.

The cry came again, this time accompanied by dragging gasps of air that crumbled into weeping sobs. It was undoubtedly the voice of Mrs. Earp coming from inside the house.

"Mrs. Earp?" I yelled.

No answer.

Now fully and horrifyingly ripped out of my daydream, I bolted inside, throwing the door open so forcefully that the ground-floor windows rattled in my wake. There was still no answer, but I could hear the unmistakable cacophony of horrible sobbing coming from the second floor. Without heeding the possibility of danger, I sprinted up the stairs and through the first open door I saw. It was the Earps' bedroom.

The old engineer lay on the floor, a pool of black liquid still spreading wide under his body. His wife was sobbing on the ground next to him, her back pressed up against the bed and her hands slowly patting Mr. Earp's head and arms as if she were trying to comfort a newborn child.

"Dear God, what happened?" I asked in shock, kneeling down to look at the wounded man's head. A long diagonal gash stretched from the top of his skull to his ear. It was bleeding, but his chest still rose and fell, though slowly. He was definitely still alive, but something or someone had attacked him. Such a cut couldn't have been done by a fall. He could not talk, and his eyes stayed welded shut. I looked around the room and noticed that the blood in the black pool of liquid was mixed with oil from a shattered lantern lying in pieces next to the bed.

"What happened?" I repeated, trying to unwrap the old man from his wife's ironlike grip so I could place him on the bed. I noticed multiple bruises also stood out on his thin forearms and face. He looked very pale.

"Those bastards! They did this! Took all our papers and money from the safe!"

"What bastards?" I asked, quickly tearing off the end of the bed sheet and wrapping it around Mr. Earp's head. I then made sure to gingerly extricate the wounded man from his grieving wife.

"Three of the countrymen and that devil, Amy! They said we owed them a debt, and that they had come to take it. Outlaws! Savages! We owed no one! Haven't for twenty years!"

"What? Amy? But she's with me. She's been with me, right here." I gestured over my shoulder, pointing with my free hand to show the distraught woman that Amy was right there behind me. But, after swinging my head round in the gesture, I realized there was no Amy. The door was a vacant hole in the universe, sable and dark in the windowless room.

"No . . . no, that's impossible. She's right down there. We've been looking for the flower up north. She couldn't have been here."

"She must have told them!" was all she shrieked. She collapsed onto the floor, sobbing even harder than before. "She told them before you left . . . she told them we were alone." I sat dumbfounded, staring at her withered form on the floor. I still held the shivering body of her husband in my arms. The slow, pitiful sobs were sequentially punctuated with waning repetitions of the horrible phrase. Bleary-eyed in my confusion, I left their side and stumbled down the stairs. The back door was still open. The windows still seemed to vibrate with the percussion of my panic until I looked out the open door at the muddy road. Then it all fell silent. The whispering wind fell dead at my feet, and the now poisonously yellow sunlight crept unimpeded into the cold living room. The road was empty.

Amy was gone.

Letter addressed to Marco Arwaldt from Dr. Charles Martins,
Editor of "The Journal of Modern Botanical Science"
Gloucester, UK
January 15, 1832

Dear Mr. Arwaldt,

I regret to inform you that The Journal cannot accept your client's manuscript as is. Besides being much longer than our general standard of conciseness requires, the work contains less than acceptable scientific value in the eyes of our reviewers.

The third section in particular lacks any discernable didactic meaning, and what little information exists is clouded by a rather obtuse exploration of creative writing. An uninformed reader might even think that the author is not writing about flowers at all.

Due to your current standing as a beneficiary and trusted agent, we are willing to extend a second review upon revision of the primary source material. The suggestion landed on by me and my peers would be the inclusion of a literature review in the third section's place, as well as an addition of labeled and measured diagrams. This would, in our opinion, improve the value of the piece.

In this vein and as a personal note, your client seems extremely interested in the field on a surface level, and even writes some stilling paragraphs of prose to describe his travels, but he has put little to no focus on the pedagogical aspect of the study. I might suggest looking into inquiries with my friend at Blackbridge. He publishes novels and stories, both fiction and nonfiction, for "The Continental," and perhaps he would enjoy your client's writings more readily than us in the scientific community. I have included his card.

    Regards,
    Dr. Martins
    Managing Editor
    The Journal of Modern Botanical Science

Letter addressed to James Torrey from Marco Arwaldt
Black Hawk, TN, USA
February 15, 1832

James,

I'm at a loss for words. I have just read your letter while in a cart on my way to a business meeting and am scribbling this reply as best I can on a spare piece of parchment. Amy, the horrific ending, the star, even the illustrations, they all leave me not knowing exactly what to say. I am sorry, truly, for the ordeal you have had to endure.

. . . Amy especially. I almost can't believe it, and I feel that there is nothing I can think or say that will relieve me or you of that dissonance. It is something, I fear, that we will frequently have to remind ourselves to forget if we are to ever get past it.

I think it might be possible that a pause would do you some good. Perhaps waiting just a while, a couple years or so, before continuing your search is something we should consider. You have gone through a lot, and these things can pile up behind a person without him realizing it.

Please consider this as clearly as you can. There is no shame in waiting a while for your health.

Write to me again as soon as you can. I will be here in Gloucester for the foreseeable future and will check my box every day. I do have some other . . . revisionary news to tell you, but I can hear my cart starting to slow, and I do not have enough time at the moment to relate it with the proper form.

I hope you are all right. If I can, I will try to arrange a trip so we can see each other in person. Write to me with your thoughts about the near future. I will be awaiting your reply from the minute this leaves my hands.

— MA

Letter addressed to Marco Arwaldt from James Torrey
Gloucester, UK
May 2, 1832

Dear Marco,
I have found a carriage at the beginning of winter.

No wasted time, though I greatly appreciate your concern. I will need your help finding a guide, but the supplies I can manage on my own this time.

I will find this one. I have to.

— James

5. The Ghostbloom Flower (*Sarcodes gelidara*)

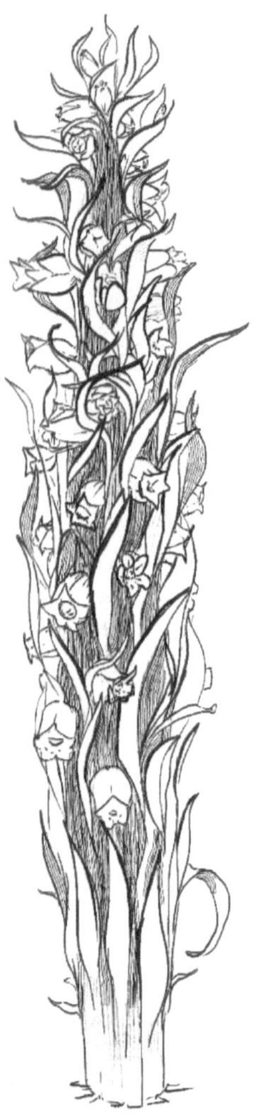

Location:

The *Sarcodes gelidara* is native to the high alpine climates of the Rocky Mountains and the rolling northern foothills of the central United States of America. While similar to its western American sister, *Sarcodes sanguinea* (which blooms in spring during snowmelt), the *S. gelidara* usually blooms about two months earlier (during the middle of winter) and does not have the red hue of its sister flower. It also cannot grow without a consistent temperature below freezing, leading to its preference for alpine territory and its peculiar frozen adornments. The plant itself grows out of fungal root systems that spread underneath the montane soil, allowing it to thrive without any direct sun or water supply. The *S. gelidara* being primarily parasitic, the presence of healthy coniferous root systems underlying the fungal ones is also necessary for the flower to grow and thrive, contributing further to its rarity. The flower is usually found in the shade of its host trees, often sprouting out of the snow to a maximum height of thirty centimeters.

Cultivation:

Ghostbloom flower cultivation has proven extremely difficult. While the flower has been shown to grow well when given a perfect environment close in humidity and temperature to frigid montane landscapes, even slight rises in temperature quickly result in wilting and death. Because of its parasitic nature, a prospective cultivator would need to grow a grove of coniferous trees preemptively, acquire a greenhouse large enough for said root system, cultivate an appropriate mycelium habitat around the roots, and regulate the temperature to below freezing without killing the coniferous trees. The flower also cannot be transplanted to a different root system, repotted, or transported, leading to its almost nonexistent appearance in botanical gardens. Needless to say, such a pursuit as reliably cultivating the *S. gelidara* would be nigh impossible with current botanical resources, though it is theoretically feasible. To date, no record of any successful cultivation attempt has been published.

Description:

The *Sarcodes gelidara* manifests as a small stalk (twenty-five to thirty centimeters) of tightly interwoven, colorless flowers. The stalks usually grow near coniferous trees, particularly cypress, and emerge out of snow-covered areas under which lie beds of decayed pines. The plant's scientific name is derived from the Latin word for ice and alludes to its strikingly white hue, which covers the entirety of the adult plant, including its roots. Additionally, due to the flower's need for subfreezing temperatures, it is common for star-like ice formations to form at the ends of its flower buds. This is primarily caused by the conical structure of the petals and gives the rather striking appearance of a small, traditionally ornamented Christmas tree.

*

Recovered entry from James Torrey's journal
Dated November 15, 1832

The last expedition weighed heavily on me, but I could not pause my inexorable plan without risking the loss of more money and time. I had just enough of each to return home again to Tennessee for a short while. The Sarcodes gelidara only grows at the beginning of winter in the northwestern mountains. A full year would need to pass before conditions would be right again if I miss this window of opportunity.

In an almost delirious state of anxiety, I even wrote a letter to Marco to ask him to accompany me. I desperately wanted a familiar face again, if only to hold onto the feelings I had briefly experienced with Amy before her disappearance. I wrote about everything. It must have taken me over an hour to write less than two pages. But after finishing it and sitting at my desk regarding it with a strange feeling of embarrassment, I became overwhelmed and stuffed it away in the bottom of my notebook case.

I never sent it, although I did end up writing a much shorter letter the day after to let him know the essentials.

I purchased a horse-drawn wagon I had found in the tiny town of Carlyle, Illinois, and picked up my new guide in the relatively adjacent town of Jeska, just over fifty miles west of the engineer's inn.

Speaking of the engineer, I left him and his wife healthy, but as poor as they had been in their entire lives and still in danger from more attacks by the bandits. The aftermath of the ordeal taught me that you are never really out of debt with bad men. I was almost sure that they would move back east to a safer area, but they would not tell me their plans or even listen to any of my suggestions — so I was forced to leave. My conscience, heavy with sadness and a feeling of powerlessness, dragged my chin down to my chest and my hat over my eyes as I packed up my belongings and headed out, back east toward home. To this day, I still do not know the truth about why Amy left. Why she did that to me. Guesses and doubts swim around my brain like cawing birds. Our talk the night before, her eager face when she asked me questions about home, her past, the drawings. What was it all for? I don't know. I might never know.

I wish I could just ask her why.

Two days into my trip toward the mountains, before I picked up my guide in Jeska, it began to snow. Big fluffy flakes drifted through the frozen air onto the brim of my hat and clung to the short hair of my horses, quickly melting from the heat of their bodies.

I had always loved snow as a child. Though it heralded a poor time for gardening, my mother made up for that with cozy nights by the fire. We were lucky enough to have a bay window on the first floor of our house with a reading seat next to it. The magic of snow from back then seemed so elusive during my time in school, but under the shade of the prairie trees, I had plenty of time to think on the subject — a necessary reprieve.

After ruminating for a while, I came to the conclusion that it must be the silence of it all. I could look up and see millions of fluttering white creatures falling from quickly passing clouds. They flowed like birds and danced in the sky above me, yet there was magically no sound, no auditory indication of action. The magic of the snow was that it confused the agreement between my eyes and ears and created a kind of surreal melancholy that even the mystical drum of rain couldn't accomplish. It was this rather whimsical realization, I believe, that really brought me out of my reverie . . . that, and my new traveling companion.

Personal Notes:

The guide I had found (or rather that Marco, again, had contacted) was an Indian of the Crow people. He was a generous fellow and surprisingly talkative. He quickly told me his Apsáalooke name, a word I could embarrassingly not pronounce. At this he did not seem surprised, and after laughing at my few clumsy attempts at recitation, told me promptly to call him by his *Baashciile* name, Swan. *Baashciile*, I learned, is what his people call the white man. Swan informed me it means "white eyes" in the Crow language.

He had brought his own cart and horses, already laden with some supplies, so I sold my new one in Jeska and piled the back of his cart with the equipment I had brought along. Together we had a full bounty of food and clothes.

I must admit I was rather nervous when approaching our rendezvous point. Upon meeting him, however, my fears were quickly dispersed. He was a short but skinny man with two long black braids tied back behind him and a puff of hair jutting up just above his forehead. Though his face was harsh and muddied by the abrasive forces of the western winter, his eyes were warm and soft, peeping brightly out from under his furrowed brow. He smiled peacefully and met my one outstretched hand with his two. We had hardly known each other for ten minutes before I had been thoroughly briefed on his life history and that of his people.

The daylong rides passed in what seemed a matter of minutes. He talked the whole time, barely letting me say a word. This I did not mind. Not only did it drag my thoughts from the bitter cold of the winter wind hitting my face, but it also filled me with confidence that Marco had chosen the right man, and the renewing effect that can only be produced by the companionship of another eccentric human being washed over me.

"We have many different flowers in Apsáalooke country, Flower Boy," he said. "*Akbaatatdía* has created many different flowers on Apsáalooke lands, found nowhere else on Grandmother Earth."

Before the first day of travel ended, he had related the beauty of the mystical coneflowers, which, he told me, wounded elk ate to cure their pains. He also told me about the medicinal yarrow, a flowering plant that his tribe used to cure everything from infection to missed menstruations. I was vaguely familiar with the plant already. It was called "bloodwort" in old English war textbooks, but I had never known that it was used to an almost comically greater effect in America. "Yarrow" was also a much better name for the flower than "bloodwort," a moniker that had always brought up horribly fungal images in my mind. This poetic language disparity was made even more evident as Swan kept adding words to the list of flowers and places for which the Apsáalooke had different names than the English settlers, and I found that I actually preferred the rather beautifully complex names of the Natives to the ones I had hurriedly scrawled in my notes while studying in school. As I was soon told, even the name of their tribe, which had been introduced to me as the callously simple "Crow people," was incorrect. An injustice that Swan immediately, though good-naturedly, rejected.

"Apsáalooke does not even mean crow," he said as we passed under a grove of prairie trees, a toothy grin spreading over his soft face and reddening it against the cold. "Do I look like a crow to you? No, Apsáalooke means . . . well, it means a great many things, but the closest you can get in your language is 'Children of the Great Bird.' Not even close to "crow"! Us, we are the children of the great Thunderbird, and grandchildren of Mother Earth."

Near the end of the long day, I learned that the *S. gelidara*'s proper name (which is to say, its primary one given by the Apsáalooke) is the *dúupuule* flower.

Needless to say, our bond grew remarkably quickly, and I ended the first day's trip at a small traveler's cabin having lost a guide and gained a friend.

*

The cabin itself was a horrid mockery of the hospitable inn I had stayed at merely a two-day's journey east. It had the dank, abandoned look of a swamp boathouse, but the freshly fallen snow made it look even more derelict and cold. One could easily see the weak points of the roof, as the smooth surface of the snow laden on its top dipped and distorted in all sorts of concerning directions. Swan seemed pleased to find it, however, and we went to work at once collecting twigs and branches to make a fire, dragging them inside the cabin's cramped—but snowless—interior.

The fire started within half an hour, and we ate our dinner hurriedly. After, with the coals still glowing orange in the night, we curled up and slept in the thick quilts we had brought with us. My thoughts again turned to flowers. I tried to picture some of the flowers Swan had mentioned during our travel. My head swam with phantasms and visions of the strangest shapes and textures I imagined a flower could produce, and these late-night imaginings crept into my dreams. Though the shack was cold, and getting colder by the minute, my mind was easily stolen by wonder, darting back and forth between tree trunks and shriveled, frozen bushes looking for the spiral stalk of the *dúupuule*.

*

We did not leave the next morning as planned. The bitter wind of the western mountains had descended upon us as we slept. The sky was completely obscured by luminous gray clouds hovering over the prairie like metallic cotton. By the time we woke and made breakfast, the snow had started to fall again. This time it came not as thick, floating flakes, but quick, tiny daggers. The wind whipped them through the trees, covering the entire left side of the house in a sharp, curving drift.

"We cannot leave today . . . or even tomorrow," said Swan that morning. "The snow will be gone when it gets more windy, but now it's going to be really cold." He shook his head as he watched the flakes.

He was right. The storm lasted two whole days, entombing us in our already collapsing cottage. During our internment, we very rarely left our fortress. When we did brave the winter winds swirling outside, it was usually only to collect more sticks for the fire. We cooked the food that we had brought, which was thankfully plentiful enough to last a couple of weeks at least. The addition of the wagon meant we were much more prepared than on my last journey, though the horses needed to be cared for as well. On the first morning of the storm, Swan told me he was very worried for their health, so he led them away from the small doorless structure that they had huddled under and inside near where we slept, sitting them by the fire and rubbing their legs with his hands.

It was apparently custom in his tribe to tell stories during these long periods of winter isolation, and the whole while I was enchanted by the amount of tales and fables he had stored in his memory, some of which were even from other tribes he had interacted with at a trading fort up north. He would talk for hours about the trees, the coyotes, benevolent and evil spirits, shapeshifters, and evil cannibalistic creatures the Cree people called *wîhtikow*. These, he told me, were the spirits of travelers who got caught in snowstorms just like this and had given in to the carnal need for survival, eating their traveling companions to survive. He told me this at night with his eyes reflecting the vivid flame of the fire (I realized afterward that this was deliberate) and then roared with laughter when he saw how terrified his story had made me.

"You are scared of too many things, Flower Boy," he said. "If I get too cold and die, you can go ahead and eat me; that way you become one of those *wîhtikow* and won't be scared of them anymore!" He laughed again, rocking back and forth with mirth.

What a horrifyingly kind thing to say, I remember thinking that night as I started to fall asleep against one of the horses, the one Swan had told me was called Sunrise in English. Her soft black pelt absorbed the radiant heat of the blaze and reflected it back into my neck and shoulders. Swan sat on the other side of the fire, curled up against the other horse, named Gale. They both started to snore in tempo as the night set in, and I could hear the slowly waning whine of the wind outside slip into silence, signaling the gradual but sure end to the storm.

*

Finally, after three days in that cold cabin, we began our trek through the sparse forest, Swan atop Sunrise and I riding Gale. The woodlands of the untamed West were much different than those off the American coast. In Maine and the blurry green of New England, forests stretch unimpeded for miles across the sloped expanse of river-crossed hills. Occasionally a large thumb of earth rises to form a smooth hillock, also covered in the slanted conifers that cloak the tors in their even emerald. In the West, however, the trees were jagged and uneven, and they only grew in the black hills of the southeastern plateaus. These arboreal fangs seemed to rise in height with the terrain. What used to be an infinite ocean of grass became a cold, snow-cloaked valley surrounded by jutting, mountainous rock. The trees also did not grow straight up into the sky, but instead jutted directly out from every vaguely horizontal surface, cutting the air at odd angles and running askance into each other.

Swan and I, having had to leave our cart at the cabin, rode the newly saddled horses over the shallow passes of the valley, cutting thin paths into the as we went. The only things I needed to carry were extra clothes for the inclement weather and enough food for myself. Swan had brought the same, with the addition of a small rifle for protection or emergency hunting. This he packed in a slanted scabbard-like fur case at the front of his saddle.

The trails, while not particularly dangerous, were far removed from any kind of civilization, and this isolation made me very weary of the treacherous terrain. Even minor injuries would make it exceedingly difficult to return to safety. The cold, however, was by far the most oppressive factor. I trusted Swan's ability to make a fire in such conditions, and he never showed any sign of being surprised at the sudden drops in temperature I felt on our way through the passes, but I could not ignore the creeping numbness that crawled between my toes and up my fingers.

Despite this, I was encouraged again by the hope of finding another one of my flowers, a feeling that had not been nearly as powerful during my last two adventures. While the path to this one was nowhere near as sure as the corpse flower or the orphan orchid, it was also not as elusive as the stylite star. It was true, there was little scientific literature about the *dúupuule*, but the Indian tribes had observed it many times and viewed it more as a winter omen than a rarity. Swan himself said he had never passed a solstice without seeing the plant in the location to which he now led me.

The place was part of a kind of isolation ritual where young Natives were taken yearly to find the requisite inner peace and natural appreciation for advancement in life. This pilgrimage was usually made in the springtime, but Swan was adamant that he had often made it with other young men when snow still caked the jagged rocks and taloned trees of the hills.

Here he, alongside these other young men, had apparently experienced what he called "the history of the world," and found the answers to many of the questions he had asked as a child. Following those lines of thought, he told me even more stories about the birds and the animals that lived in the cold frontier.

Near the middle of our first day after the storm, he recounted that on his first trip here, he had learned about the spirits of Thrown-in-Spring and Thrown-behind-Curtain.

A mother, pregnant with twin boys, was attacked one night by an enemy that Swan only called "The Red Woman." This witch-like figure killed the mother and ripped the unborn twins from her womb. The first child she threw into a corner of the room, and the second she dragged outside and threw in a nearby spring. These misfortunes gave them their names. The children, spirits at first, were eventually brought back to life by their returning father, who coaxed them back into the land of the living through incense and trickery. These twins went on many adventures together, including a horrifying journey into a misty valley in between the very same mountains that Swan was guiding me to. This valley had apparently been occupied by a massive alligator-like snake that had terrorized the area for an untold amount of time. The creature lured the boys into the misty vale during a particularly dark night. As it slithered around them, trying to lull them to sleep, the boys heard its beating heart in the middle of its body. Fighting against its soporific power, they managed to wake each other up, and, using a knife their father had given them, cut out the creature's heart. This act of justice made the valley safe to travel for everyone, including us.

"Sometimes," said my guide with a wan smile, "you can still hear that slow beat of that beast's heart in the mountain fog. They say it gets slower ever since its defeat, but still, it does not stop."

I found the story fantastic, but my confusion at its overall message was strong. At the end of his recital, I asked Swan, "What is the meaning of all these scary stories? Why would they tell you this—and when you were a child no less?"

Swan thought for a while, then answered in a steady and resolved tone. "It is for when someone looks at the valleys of the lands and . . . and asks, 'Why?'"

The distracting power of the statement carried my thoughts through the entire rest of that evening, and before I knew it, we were only a day's ride from where the *dúupuule* grew.

*

The last leg of the journey was by far the most treacherous. The jagged rocks slowly transformed into solid-red cliffs, their sheer, vertical surfaces rust-like against the pale snow. It stormed that last day as well, adding more and more weight to each of the horses' heavy steps. The deceivingly smooth blanket of snow that covered the trail hid the uneven path underneath. Progress was slow, but steady and sure. There was a lull in Swan's storytelling corresponding with what I assumed was an increase in necessary concentration. We drifted into a period of complete, yet tense silence. I unconsciously trusted his judgment and found my mind wandering off into a fatigue-driven daydream. At times, the whole gale went silent to my ears. I watched the snow fall overhead and melt into the mane of my horse. My mind flitted back and forth trying to find something to concentrate on besides the biting cold and the infinite white of the path.

Almost two hours after we had broken down our camp, we encountered a thin, steeply banked outcrop at the end of a series of grueling switchbacks. The wind and snow had let up a little, and we could tell the sun lay somewhere beyond the sheet of steel-gray clouds above us. As we rounded the corner of the outcrop, Sunrise stumbled suddenly to the right. The rocky slope of the ledge we had been navigating swung her out to the side and unbalanced her. For several heavy seconds, Swan's arms jutted out in the opposite direction, attempting to counteract the shift in weight, but his pack was too heavy, and his hands grasped uselessly at the reins. His horse's back hips sank diagonally downward as her right hind leg kicked out into open space, and her whole body began to slide over the edge. Swan's shoulders wobbled as he started to fall with the struggling body underneath him. A piercing whinny shot through the air as the horse's head jerked up and to the left. I could see her wide white eyes flash in panic. I had barely begun to shout my surprise when, with a fierce grunt of effort, Swan leaned violently to the left and caught the bottom buckle of the saddle in his hand and heaved. Though the horse's right foot pawed franticly, useless in the air, the force Swan had exerted weighted its left side, digging the horse deeper into the soft snow. Slowly, under the balanced pressure of her rider and cargo, Sunrise straightened her left leg, and Swan hauled himself back up to a neutral position. The right hind leg regained a foothold, and the horse trotted forward out of danger.

With a cunning smile, Swan looked back at me and said, "Almost needed to pray to those twins. A shame that would have been. I heard they died fifty winter storms ago."

Still slightly shocked, I could only exhale my anxiety into a half-sigh of relief. Recovered, we continued around the curve of the mountain path in a much less quiet silence than before.

It was evening before we got to the spot Swan had talked about. As we rounded the final diagonal switchback, a gust of glacial wind blasted over the edge of the precipice, flurrying the mane of my horse. Fighting against it, we finally broke over the drift of snow at the top and into a beautiful pale clearing surrounded by a menacing fence of knifing red rocks. The landing was completely flat and remained so for about thirty meters before narrowing into another trail that continued across the mountainside. At the base of the clearing, nearest the rocky wall, was a small frozen pond; a creeping river extended from its lowest point toward the edge, making its way down to the valley below. Next to the pond grew a tall, sloping pine tree that bent forward over the ice under the weight of its fresh mantle of snow. The middle of the clearing contained numerous knee-high boulders arranged in a circle that looked like they were meant to be sat upon. I could almost imagine Swan sitting here with a ring of young Apsáalooke men in a familial circle.

After surveying the scene, I got off my horse and secured her to a nearby tree, one of the few growing out of the thin montane soil alongside the tall pine. Carefully, I crept back and forth over the white clearing, scanning for the curling buds of the ghostbloom flower.

I started at the water's edge and circled outward. Though the water was frozen, the fact that the flower grew parasitically off of conifer roots meant that where there were roots, there could be blooms, and the tree roots closest to water were the most likely to thrive. Though this did give me a statistically higher likelihood of finding the flower in that area, success was by no means certain, and it was apparent that the task of surveying even this small area carefully was going to take some time.

Swan helped me, looking over the snowy rocks with a practiced eye and checking specific areas that he remembered from before. I had been told that the plant's early growth usually punched its way through the snow like a bamboo shoot before showing any serious kind of bloom, but finding these would not do me any good. I was looking to record and describe the flower itself, not its half-grown sprout. I needed to see it in bloom.

I crawled back and forth for almost two hours before tiring and taking a break. From the low position of the sun, I could tell that we had just over an hour of daylight left, and I had only succeeded in combing half of the area. Despite this, neither Swan nor I had found much, only once finding a short grayish bud of the aforementioned seedling with no bloom.

Nevertheless, this discovery gave me hope. The existence of a seedling confirmed the presence of both the roots and the proprietary fungi that they stole nutrients from, and I was as confident as ever that a bloom was somewhere to be found nearby.

"There is one more spot I want to check quick before dark," Swan told me, saddling up his horse again. "There is an open area just over there. I have seen some of your flowers there before. If I do not see anything, we will camp here." I reluctantly agreed; I was tired by the long day's ride and our so far fruitless search but decided to trust Swan's intuition.

The path toward the next landing was even thinner than the previous few. It was also angled down, curving to the right around the widening base of the mountain. It was made even more difficult by low rock overhangs jutting out of the slope above us; they posed no obstacle for the horses, but a great obstacle for their riders. I found myself tilting awkwardly to the left to avoid hitting my head on the cold red roof, which caused me to teeter dangerously over the sheer slope of the mountain.

The path contained numerous steep switchbacks, and we passed the silver vein of the descending frozen river more than five times as we crossed back and forth. As the path slowly started to level out, I heard a light tap to my right. I looked in the direction of the sound and, seeing a newly formed dark stain on my saddle, realized a large droplet of water had struck and melted into the tanned leather.

My horse stopped for a second, attempting to navigate a particularly sharp turn onto the next slope, and I used the pause to look up at the wall of rock next to me. Above hung a long, thin icicle, clearly a product of the meandering alpine river originating from the pool we had seen at the top. The long finger of ice had a small amount of water coating its surface, and a large droplet had dripped off and been the cause of my distraction. The strange notion instantly popped into my head that what I had thought had been a deep freeze of the water's current was actually just superficial. The water must indeed be flowing under the ice and slowly making its way down the mountain despite the frigid temperature of the area.

Then, what had seemed a blissfully distant possibility soon jumped into sudden reality. From in front of me, I heard Swan scream: the thick, yelling scream of a fully grown man, accompanied shortly after by the fierce whinny of his horse. My head could not turn fast enough to match my mounting panic, and by the time I finally focused my eyes on the scene in front of me, Swan and Sunrise were already over the edge. Tufts of snow were thrown into a floating flurry as his horse's hooves scrambled in a vain attempt to maintain traction, the pair leaving a ghostly cloud of frost in their wake. As the panicked animal searched for purchase where there was none, the rest of the snow bluff blew away under them, and they both tumbled out of my view in unison.

Shocked, I yelled and immediately jumped off my horse. I ran the short distance to the edge of the slope and leaned my head over. Swan had fallen out of the saddle as they descended, and the pair had left a wake of malicious-looking broken branches and disturbed rocks that blocked my sight. I ran down the trail with my horse behind me, trying to get a better view of their fall. Through the oil-black maze of ice-cloaked trees, my eyes followed the trail quickly, searching and finally landing on the tan color of Swan's leather coat. He was lying motionless at the bottom of the valley, half-submerged in a newly opened crack in the ice of the stream descending from above. The creek, as it fell over the cliff and into the valley, expanded into a wicked river that flowed through the now-visible vale. I could not see his horse through the narrow corridor of broken branches. With painful, anxious caution, I maneuvered Gale past the slippery ice of the remaining switchbacks. Remounting, I started down the final slope, traveling as fast as I could. It was a full five minutes before I was able to make it to the valley floor.

Spotting Swan again as I reached level ground, I spurred my horse over to where he lay; he was still partially submerged in the deadly water. Yelling his name as if he were half-deaf, I dismounted and pulled him out onto the wet snow.

"Swan." I said, barely able to speak through my heavy breaths of effort. "Swan, are you all right?" His brow was furrowed in pain, but the low groan he made in reply told me he was still conscious. He tugged feebly at the glove of his left hand, which I only then realized was covered in blood. "What's hurt?" I half shouted to him, my breath blasting out in swirling clouds that encircled his head.

He pointed with his right hand. When my eyes focused again, I saw it. From the center of his left wrist emerged the bloody end of a sharp stick, jutting straight out from his forearm. The wound looked horrible in its clarity. Little blood had seeped out, but the injury's devastating consequence was still fully visible. To make things worse, the entire left half of his body had been thrown against the ice, shattering the thin layer on top and plunging his leg, arm, and shoulder into the freezing water. His clothes were soaked. Having been incapacitated by shock, Swan had been unable to move until I got to him. His left arm had been fully submerged for the entire time it had taken me to ride down.

Still dazed, he did not resist when I helped him to sit up. I attempted to pull him farther away from the water onto a nearby rock to get his coat off, but as I did this, he made a panicked grunting sound and shook me off with a violent jerk. He let out a jagged breath and, releasing his hold on his injured arm, used his right hand to point past my head.

"Sunrise," he gasped out with a shudder.

I looked behind me. Swan's horse had been lying further downstream. I hadn't noticed her in my panic to attend to Swan, deaf as I was with anxiety and fear. As I looked at her, I realized she was in a great deal of danger and pain. Her body was half-submerged in a broken section of river, and she had thrashed about, attempting to right herself. As if realizing my observance, she let out a piercing whinny filled with fear and desperation.

I immediately ran toward her. She saw me coming and began to twist and turn with even more excitement. She was obviously injured in some way, and this instinctive movement had a disastrous effect. Her batting hind legs broke even more of the thin ice of the river behind her, shattering what little traction on the shore she had left. She stumbled again, plunging deeper and deeper into the water. I could see the flow of the river beneath the ice as more of the sheet cracked and broke free.

A loud snap rent the air. A large fissure sprang into existence, bisecting the whole river.

Even as I ran, I could tell it was over for the horse. Her front left leg was visibly crippled, and the way her rear hoofs powerlessly pawed backward at the water meant that her back legs were injured as well, but it didn't occur to me what needed to be done until I was already halfway to the dying steed.

I stopped fast in the snow, my boots leaving long trenches as they slid to a halt. The thing that had caught my eye was the crumpled saddle. It lay just a meter to my right, the empty scabbard still lashed to the leather.

The gun.

My anxiety growing more and more entropic, I turned around. I could see Swan still sitting where I had set him, but his uninjured hand was now pointing feebly to his left; a dark spot blotched the crystal white of the surrounding snow. The gun must have slipped from the holster as Swan had fallen. He had known the horse's necessary fate as soon as he pointed me to the animal but had been unable to communicate the truth to me in his dazed state. I bolted back towards the dark outline, taking long, powerful strides through the already hole-speckled snow.

Reaching the naked weapon, I picked it up and turned back toward the screaming animal, only to see that I was too late.

The crack cutting the river in half had grown into a massive fissure, starting from the hole where the horse had landed and scattering in a thousand directions downstream. Still, I started running again, frustration now pushing me backward through my footsteps. I tore after the sinking animal, the cold metal of the gun burning my hand to numbness.

I stopped before getting even halfway back. One final whinny cut the air before the shining head of the horse descended under the water, the once-sturdy steed unable to keep her body afloat.

Without knowing it, I sank to the ground. My knees fell feebly into the first set of tracks I had cut like craters in the snow.

Partially recovered entry from

James Torrey's journal

No date given

Dear Marco,

I used to write to you a lot in college. You may not understand me when I say that, but it is true. I just never sent the letters. I had another, more interesting journal back then, and I would write many letters in it, none of which survived my education I'm afraid. I burned it before our graduation. My dramatic streak was just as alive back then as it is now.

I am writing this letter, another one which I'm sure I will not send, for a reason, though. I have something to tell you. A confession, actually. Recently, I have found myself overwhelmed at times, and the only thing I can think to do is write. It's all I've ever done when faced with difficulties, and I am no more courageous now than I was in our school days. So, I will take the way of the coward's pen, and write you a letter you will never read. How sad it sounds when I put it like that.

This confession comes from 1825 or 26. I can't pin it down exactly. Whenever I try and telescope in on the day, it vanishes from my focus, and then all of a sudden, all of my school days appear as one homogenous fog. Regardless, I do remember that it was not raining that evening, but the wind was cold and horrid.

This school day had finished with the end of my afternoon class. I was walking out of Arber Hall, wrapping my coat and scarf tightly around me as the wind blasted past the building's stone pillars.

It was a Friday then, and my afternoon classes were all that occupied me before the weekend. As you know, I was practically a recluse on our days off, and I planned to be one this specific weekend as well. However, I did have plans for that night. A girl named Alex who worked around the town had asked me to go to a bar after classes finished.

I remember that, just as I walked out of the building that afternoon, I felt a tiny tap on my shoulder. I almost thought it was the wind again, it was so light, but a small peep of a voice caught my attention, and I turned back toward the building. Alex was there, curled around her Latin books. Latin classes were important to us back then, weren't they? I recall you always seemed to have that one text, "Historium Naturalis" or something like that, by Martius, in your arms. Alex, if I remember, wasn't even a student at the school, but she loved to sit and listen to the lectures if the teachers let her. I heard the librarian at the college had given her the Latin book after seeing her come in so many times to sit with us and listen. I guess I never really thought about how strange that was to us, that she couldn't just go to school in the same way. We were all so young back then.

"Oh . . . Alex," was all I could think to say. It came out in a stutter, which I hoped sounded like it came from the cold.

She looked nervous. Her short, tightly curled hair sprung out from the back of the red winter hat that was folded over her ears. With my equally awkward greeting, she seemed to gain confidence again.

"James . . . will I still see you at the Blue Bell tonight?" she asked very softly. Her blue eyes blinked wide at me. Her mouth twitched after the question as if to find something else to say.

To my great embarrassment to this day, I didn't hear her completely over the wind, and turned my head to the side so as to block the roar of the weather with the back of my ear. In this awkward, diagonal position, I said, "What was that?"

Of course, it was at this moment that my brain finally caught up to the situation, and just as it clicked into place, I started to say, "Oh! Yes of course! The bar!" and accidentally talked over her as she started to repeat her original query in answer to mine.

There are some . . . no, many moments in my life that I fear have condemned me to eternal embarrassment, and I have decades of sleepless nights to look forward to, no doubt. This was one of those moments, and I stared dumbly at her in the following empty seconds.

"Uh . . . um," was all I could get out to break the hanging silence between us. In that moment, the wind, probably feeling bad for both of us, blew past in a large gust, almost toppling me over onto the concrete steps. She, being guarded somewhat by the doorway which she was still half-way inside, survived the blast; her hat was the only casualty, as it was flung off her head and landed on the ground at my feet.

The wind died down again after a moment or two. Thankful for the opportunity to place my eyes elsewhere, I stooped down and picked up the fallen garment. I then held it out to her.

Her previously rumpled hair had flown out, and her springy curls were now bobbing up and down in the slantways push of the receding breeze. She smiled as she took it back. Her eyes were directed at the blank space just to the left of my feet.

"Thank you . . .," she said. "I'll see you there at six?"

That's when you arrived.

"James!" came your breathless voice through the rustling sound of the surrounding trees. I turned and saw you running full tilt toward me across the green. "James! There you are! I've been looking all over campus for you! Why weren't you in your room?"

"I had class today till four," I replied to your hunched-over form, surprised at your uncharacteristically flustered appearance. You looked like you really had run all over campus. "You know that, Marco."

"Right, right," you said, standing up straight again and brushing invisible dust from the front of your long coat. Between gasping breaths, you continued. "I . . . have something I need you to do for me . . . I'm in a little bit of a bind, you see."

It was then that I remembered Alex and looked back to the doorway where she had been. It lay empty, the yellow tile of the hall beyond glistening with the reflection of the softened daylight behind me. She had vanished into thin air like a ghost. How did she do that, Marco? It was like she blew away with the wind.

Your hand gripped my shoulder, and my attention was drawn back in front of me. A fluttering ball of paper had materialized on my chest.

"I don't have much time. The cart for the North trip should have left five minutes ago, and Professor Bartosz is reluctantly holding it for me."

I shuddered at that name. Bartosz, a towering sentinel of a man, was the Polish teacher who was notorious for his strict adherence to a schedule. The fact that you had gotten any kind of mercy for being late was surely a testament to his proprietary fondness for you.

With this last statement, you pressed the handful of paper to my chest even harder, almost pushing me over.

"I need you to take this and post it today. It's my application to Dublin! The last day to submit to their correspondent in the city is Wednesday, and there is only one more horse bound for New York before then! I would have obviously sent it sooner, but my friend from the city promised to take it for me tomorrow, and he has fallen ill. I just received a letter from him at noon."

You remember the Dublin letter, don't you? You were so excited to apply to work in the embassy. I remember you telling me it was the best opportunity you could have hoped for to work in the foreign mission trade. Bartosz had found you a correspondent, another show of his uncharacteristic favoritism. It was a new thing, back then, to apply for a diplomacy from a school. I do remember how excited you were, no doubt imagining yourself as an ambassador.

"When does it leave? And from what office?" I asked in haste, glancing at my watch.

"No station — the last official post office run was at two. We'll have to use a private postman." You said it all in one breath, puffs of air buffeting my face. "There is a small inn and post office called the Franklin House. It's just a mile north of here on Everton Street. Follow Division and it will be on your left, can't miss it."

"When does it leave?"

Your hand gripped my shoulder tight with this last question, and you lifted your dilated eyes to mine.

"Four thirty."

I glanced at my watch again. My eyes widened.

"Marco, it's just past four fifteen."

That moment was very strange. You must have felt it too. Your grip was just a little too strong on my shoulder, and there was a wild look in your eyes that I can't quite explain. It wasn't an angry or a panicked look. It was more regretful. Maybe sad is the word.

We stood there in inexplicable silence as the wind rumbled by again in another billowing gust. Your long coat swung to and fro, batting slightly against my left pant leg. It was only a second before you finally mastered yourself and nodded once, your mouth tightening in a familiar determination.

"Do what you can, James . . . please."

And then you were off, sprinting like an athlete across the cobblestone walkway toward the carriage station, leaving me standing with the wad of papers rustling at my chest.

So I ran too. And this, I'm afraid, is the part that is hard to tell.

*

My yellow smooth-soled shoes slid over the dirt road as I ran. Our school shoes were not really what you would call athletic wear. The clouds remained gray and formless

115

above me, and the wind pushed back and forth as I ran, sometimes nudging me along the street toward the edge of town and other times bending against me. Your letters, clutched in my hand, slapped over my knuckles as my arms swung wildly up and down. Occasionally I would stop and catch my breath, almost crumpling them on my knees as I hunched over.

Slowly, the brick buildings of the surrounding town fell away from my crunching footfalls. The ditches on the side of the road widened and became bordered by ill-defined lines of inkberry shrubs. Trees, too, stretched jaggedly and irregularly up to the sky on either side of me. The black bark and white shrub leaves all blurred together into a gray flurry that flew backward as I ran. The only point I could focus on was the thinning road. The curl of the rural lane steepened as the mile stretched on. A hill appeared, and then another. I leaned forward, bending with the angle of the small slopes and practically falling down them as they degraded. I couldn't help it at one point, and as I paused for breath a final time, I checked my watch again.

Four twenty-seven.

"I must be close," I thought. "I wasn't that slow, was I? People could run miles in six minutes or so back home — granted, not in school clothes and dress shoes."

Then I saw it. As I crested a final hillock, the tall black building standing stark and wide at the end of the turn swam into view. I panicked then, as I could not see the carriage that would take the mail. Was I too late? Did they leave early on Fridays? The whole situation flashed before my eyes. All at once I imagined walking back, not even having the power to tell you of the failure until your return. I imagined writing that night to confess and tell you that I had really tried my best.

But no! There it was. Just as my stride had slowed in despair, the carriage itself rolled out from behind the building's corner. The horses looked sable and clean, and the postman stopped the cart just outside the building. I watched as he dismounted and went inside to collect the letters.

Relief poured over me, and I picked up my pace once more, excitement pooling again in my brain. I looked at the papers as I ran and saw that a small amount of mud specks had splattered across them, but they were still very clear and proper. I feebly tried to brush the specks away with my hand, and in the process caught sight of the words you had written on the page.

"Pleased to depart by the end of the month," was all I saw.

And with that, I stopped, skidding to a halt on the loose country road. The tiny flecks of mud came off easily as I brushed them with my sleeve, leaving the paper mostly unblemished in my hands. But that's the thing, Marco. After I had the paper clean and bright . . . I didn't keep walking.

My brain reeled forward again into the future. I saw a letter returning in a week or two. I saw your happy face and smile; I heard your thanks and praise for my good deed in your time of need. I heard the school postmaster give you the letter and offer congratulations. I heard myself offer mine.

And like that, I was rooted to the spot. It was as if a winding tree trunk had sprouted from the ground in seconds and wrapped itself around my legs. The ideas in my mind echoed back and forth, shooting this way and that behind my eyes, but my shoes refused to move.

"Click," went the latch of the door to the post office. The postman came out carrying a large leather sack of papers. He hadn't seen me in the road.

Still I stood. Still I stared.

He flipped the bag onto the back of the cart, right behind the driver's seat. Then he hauled himself up and tucked his coat behind him.

The reins looked so tiny, so powerless from that distance, like they were gossamer. How could things so little and light direct letters and people so far away?

The cords snapped lightly as he flicked his hands, and the steeds trotted forward, turning away from me under the unequal pressure of his guiding tugs. Before long the carriage disappeared around the corner . . . gone . . . out of reach.

The quiet of the darkening afternoon returned. The trees seemed to stretch taller at the corners of my vision. The sun had dipped low over the horizon, peeking just under the distant stretching ceiling of the warped gray cloud.

I made it in time, Marco, but I didn't deliver your letter. That's why you didn't get accepted to Dublin. That's why the answer never even came.

*

I didn't walk back right away. It took another five minutes after the carriage had vanished from view for my heels to loosen from their binds. Then, instead of turning and just walking back, I stepped forward, your letter crumpling in my hand. I walked straight past the post office. I continued down the lane, not turning where the carriage had turned, but remaining true to the northward heading I had been following before.

Naked branches swooped at me as I walked, their gnarled fingers whipping back and forth as they caught and released the unstable breeze. The wind grew again, and it pulled at my cheeks like innumerable icy wires. I shrugged into a shiver and pulled my collar together in front of my mouth.

I wish I could describe to you the feelings that swam through my mind after that. I was angry at myself, certainly, but I also found myself troubled by a bleak recognition that I could never have sent your letter. I think I knew it the minute you handed it to me. I had been whirled away by feelings of panic and sadness for you and your position, of course, but that selfish resolution clicked into place somewhere in the dark corners of those feelings. Your goals, all the things you had told me about, everything you had worked so hard for, weren't worth you going away. Not to my selfishness.

How childish I was back then. How childish I am now, really. And look at us today, halfway across the world from each other, and I still send you letters asking about silly things like food rations and ports. You ended up leaving anyway. Nothing could stop you, and I knew that back then too, but I guess something in me also knew that I couldn't be the one to send you away.

*

I must have wandered about for almost two hours, following the rectangular circuits of the country roads as they cut through the surrounding farmland. Small, abandoned farmhouses stood like scarecrows out beyond the roads. Jagged, incomplete fences slowly faded into the ground. Eventually, I turned around and started the walk back. Dusk had fallen by then, but the wind had died down, so I wasn't as cold. My poor yellow shoes were caked in gray mud, and my returning footfalls felt infinitely heavier than the panicked steps I had taken when I ran away from the school. By the time I returned to a more municipal part of the county, the lamplighter had already come out. Small flames of light burned blurrily through the dark, and I started to dodge the mud puddles I could now see clearly. I followed the road for another half mile, down into the busier district close to the school. There I could hear the faint hum of music coming from inside one of the lit shops.

I stopped in my tracks, my memory striking me like a slap to the face.

Alex, at the Blue Bell!

I had forgotten it in my reverie. So much time wasted wandering around the bleak country. I looked up at the bright sign over the building in front of me from which the music had come. Sure enough, the vivid azure image of a dinner bell stood out like the beam of a blinding lighthouse. I yanked out my watch and held it close to my face, tilting it so it caught the sparkle of the nearest lamppost.

The delicate hands pointed at the cold black numerals, vivid against the white backplate: seven and four.

I debated. I couldn't go in, could I? I was over an hour late. Alex wouldn't even be there. What if other people were there too? I couldn't talk to them. I didn't have the energy. Best just to walk by. Don't even look inside.

All these thoughts spun through my head, winding me up like a spool of string. Slowly, carefully, I took a step forward, resolved to pass by the building as fast as I could without looking too suspicious. Both the bar's windows and door were open, no doubt to invite in potential customers who walked past.

I shoved my hands in my pockets, wishing I had horse blinders on my hat. Quickly, I shuffled past the first window. I almost thought about stopping despite my resolution, but realized how strange that would be. The last thing I should do was give whoever might be inside a chance to perceive me. Faster was better, so I kept walking. I passed the door, the tall whine of the piano growing and receding with my pace. Then the last window. I continued, but alas, my fortitude was not strong enough. At the last moment, right before I was to pass beyond the rectangular pillar of light streaming from inside, I looked to my left. It was only a dart, barely even half a second, but it was too much.

I saw her, her mass of soft, curled brown hair catching the light of the tavern's fire. Her dark green coat was hooked around the back of her chair, and she was looking right at the door I had just passed. Then, just before the half second ended, I saw her sad, squinting gaze dart over to mine. Our eyes met, but I did not stop. As soon as I passed the window, I broke into a ridiculous run, like a child running from a monster in the dark before diving under the bedcovers.

My momentum stirred up the wind again as I ran, and the cool cuts of icy air stung the corners of my eyes. My breath became jagged with the effort. My feet started to hurt, but I kept going, not even stopping to wipe my face as I felt the thin strips of tears curve over my cheeks. Before long I finally made it to my residence. In a whirl I slammed the door and fell into bed, muddy shoes and all, the prospect of the coming week looming over me like a shade. I must have cried myself to sleep that night, but I don't remember much after entering my room. The pent-up pressure of two monumental failures in almost as many hours was too much for me back then, and I think writing about it is the only thing making it bearable for me to remember today.

*

The branches of pine trees hung over us in a dark blur as I spurred Gale back up the trail. Careful not to befall the same fate as Swan and plunge him further into danger on our return, I started to ascend the hill. I was still unsure of exactly what should be done. Swan was in pain—I could tell from the aching groans that escaped his mouth. He was sitting as best he could behind me as we rode, holding onto my coat with his good hand. The only thing I could think to do was return to the clearing and start a fire. The journey back to Jeska was too long to begin right away. It would take three days of sleepless nights to get to a doctor, and I dared not ride unguarded at night in those mountainous areas. It would be far too dangerous. Getting to the cottage in less than a day and a half might be feasible if we moved fast, but that idea ran into another issue: We could not hurry. We were trapped by the mountain and the encroaching night. Perhaps we could continue north. Swan might know of an encampment there. After all, hadn't he said he had walked here with a group of kids for their pre-spring ritual? I prepared the question when, for the second time, I heard Swan's pained voice yell out.

A pang of weightlessness struck me, and the feeling of his hand on my right side vanished. Horrified, I turned around to see that Swan had thrown himself violently off the horse and back into the frozen snow. He was kneeling, but upright, his left arm still cradled to his chest, the other holding his torso off the ground. He looked up at me, and to my astonishment, a gentle expression broke over his face.

"Flower Boy, look," he said in a feeble voice, nodding his head to a spot under his shivering frame.

Directly under his body stood the pale helix of the ghostbloom flower, barely visible in the fading light. Its tuft of bright fibrous petals poked out of the snow almost a foot high, and the whole thing was encased in its rare raiment of icy baubles. Its white stalks curled around each other and ended in tens of cottony buds, which were almost fungus-like in their bulbous spirals. In the fuzzy approach of night's darkness, the plant almost looked fake, like a papier-mâché caricature of a phalangeal appendage pushing itself through a sheet of white wool.

I do not know what it was about that moment, but something in my mind flipped. Perhaps it was my concern for Swan's safety, the bitter cold of the oncoming night, or the piling stress of the whole day mounting to a peak. I cannot tell, but I was suddenly gripped by a strange sensation of anger. As I stared briefly at the feather-like plant jutting out of the snow, I could only think of how horrible it looked, like the finger of a devil. What had previously seemed like a children's imitation of a plant turned instantly into the spore of a spreading rot, stealing all of the energy it needed from the conifer roots below it.

"I don't care about the flower. Leave the damned thing here. We need to go—to get you warm."

Swan's brow furrowed. He did not answer. Instead, he just looked back down at the plant in silence. This cast me even deeper into exasperation. I threw myself off my horse, trod quickly up to his side, and started pulling him up under his shoulder.

"For God's sake Swan. Leave the flower. We need to leave now."

Swan's elbow struck me in the chest, surprising me utterly. He collapsed again from weakness on the snow, still directly above the flower.

Rattled, I stumbled back a pace or two and wrinkled my eyes in frustration. This feeling, however, instantly faded upon seeing my friend's face. He looked back at me, not in anger or irritation, but with the shockingly gentle brown eyes of empathy, the smooth skin of his face unblemished by the emotions that had so contorted mine. His eyes dipped down toward the snow. My anger melted as quickly as it had mounted.

Slowly, he got up, cradling his arm as he walked toward our horse. He didn't look back once.

I followed. I felt sick in the silence but was unsure what to say or how to say it. He mounted, still in silence, and even spurred the horse with his boot heels to set it trotting again after I had gotten on. Uneasily, my thoughts and emotions tumbled back on themselves. I snuck a couple looks at him as our pace quickened. The auburn color had drained from his face. It was as if he was fading into the tundra behind him.

A full fifteen minutes passed before he spoke again. To my shock and relief, he spoke in his usual soft and kind tone.

"It is cold, isn't it."

It was both a question and a statement. I didn't know what to say, so I said nothing, and for the rest of the journey back, we rode in the heavy winter silence of the montane snow.

*

We did not make it all the way. Halfway up, the frigid wind of the night almost blew us again off the edge. I pressed on for another minute or so, but stopped at the end of a series of switchbacks where there was a small flat recess just large enough for a campfire and tent. The storm that had erupted earlier returned as dusk approached. It did not abate after night fell, but blew flurries past our hideaway, eddying itself into our circle of light and endangering the fire I had cobbled together.

I had dressed Swan's wound as best I could before leaving the site of the accident, and he sat nursing it as I cooked a small dinner. The fire was blazing by the time we finished eating, and I kept piling more and more wood onto it. The heat drove away the numbing cold, but my brain was still reeling from the day. I felt like my breathing would not slow down, no matter how long I sat. Just sitting and staring at the fire, I tried fiercely to calm down, but to no avail. A lump in my throat pounded up and down, and my shoulders rose and fell with every sporadic deep breath. My heartbeat thumped in my chest, and I coughed out at times, my breath pluming in a mist over the blaze.

We had barely spoken since his fall. Swan seemed reservedly focused, concentrating on treating his grievous injury. After eating, I rewrapped it in a more substantial shred of cloth from my pack, leaving the stick still planted in the wound. He sat at the fire, slowly rocking the injured limb back and forth in front of the flame, occasionally wincing from the pain as the flames returned his nerves to life.

I was focused too, but my concentration was motionless. I sat opposite Swan, leaning against my pack. My mind dodged back and forth throughout the day, searching for something, anything I could have done differently. The climb, the pond, the one extra stop, the icicle omens, the river, Swan's fall, the horse, the gun, it all swam in front of me. Like a tide, memory after memory fell back in on itself as it reached its conclusion and restarted once again. I could tell that the horse dying had been the part that had unwound me, but my mind refused to stop at that point. Even after reliving getting Swan out of the snow and onto the surviving horse, my brain still pressed on, rushing past the turning point of resignation. Instead of ending the memory, it clung to every jolt—every jump and stagger of my steed on the way back up the mountain—until the final one, when Swan had pushed himself off and fallen protectively over the . . .

"You are thinking of that horse."

Swan's voice jerked me out of my memory. It had come suddenly and without identifiable tone. He had stopped rocking his arm and was looking at me with warm, wide eyes, the reflection of the fire giving them striking depth and radiance.

"Yes, you are. Well, do that. I think that will do us good."

I started to say something, the words of a half-formed apology in my head, when Swan held his finger to his lips in response, stopping me before I could get a word out.

"No, quiet for a moment. Let us think together, remember this day as one."

I blinked, and then sat back in silence, looking at my friend's illuminated face, which was surrounded by the darkened forest and skyline behind him.

"I messed up: did not realize that the path was going to be like that. I fell. You followed, worried about me. Now, as I lay at that bottom, not even sure where I was, my horse fell down that river. That horse was raised by my family, so it never got hurt before, and got scared after we fell."

This made my head lower. My mind returned back to the almost human scream of the horse as it thrashed in the ice.

Swan continued.

"You helped me get out of that water first, but I see that you did not think about that horse yet. She was gone though, at that point, because of her broken legs. I knew she would not make it." The wind whistled as he paused for breath, another wince flashing across his face for only a second.

"But you never heard that, though, because I couldn't talk. Then after a little bit you knew I wanted you to get that gun that fell and pass that horse on. Too late, though. Then that water took her away."

He winced again, still looking over the fire at me. The pain was making it difficult for him to speak. His finger had returned to his lips but was now pressed against them in a contemplative mood. The silence was widened by the snow, which deadened the eddying gusts of wind that faded over the edge of the mountain.

My eyes slid around the campsite, not sure where to focus, but I then realized Swan had raised his good hand to show his palm, lifting it just barely above his shoulder before slapping it down on his knee and making a small smacking sound.

"But we cannot stop there." he said. "No, that leads to the unknown, and the mind runs wild where it cannot get ground. That horse . . . she went down that river when it broke through. You see it as a bad thing, I can see. But that is only because her panic and cries were the last thing you saw and heard. Even though that was the last thing we see, it was not the end. The horse went under that water. She left us. Then, she flowed down deeper. The current carries her to the middle of the stream. She starts to float below the ice."

With this, Swan turned his head and held his good arm out over the sloping side of the trail, catching the wind in a cupped hand and letting the blustery snowflakes collect on his coat sleeve.

"You think of the cold as a painful thing. It stings and kills and that is it. We feel it all over our fingers and toes, up our arms and on our necks when we ride. It bites. It hurts. But this is not all that cold does. It is not how that cold kills."

He withdrew his hand and held it palm out toward the fire. The flakes quickly melted into the leather of his jacket, sparkling faintly like stars.

"After that horse went under that water, her legs and head will feel like bird talons. They will sting and burn with the ice, and it will hurt a lot. But wait just one moment more.

It is farther along the river now. The blood in the legs and feet disappears. The skin feels no more. Her head becomes heavy, thoughts slow down. The cries stop. By the time the horse reaches the bend in the river, all the pain is gone."

He brought his arm back to the injured limb and cradled it again. His eyes glided from my face to the surrounding forest, watching the snow twirl with the nighttime breeze. We fell into silence, the wandering wind muted by the quiet pressure of the coming southern squall.

"There are many things in that cold water, but panic is not one of them. It goes out through a door, like a friend when the time has come to leave. We should not ask it back."

Swan lost his hand. The doctor in Jeska had to cut it off just after the elbow.

I had ridden as fast as I could through the snowy forests and across the open plains in the preceding days, leaving Swan's cart behind near the old collapsing shack, but it had not been enough to save the limb. It is strange how I feel as I look back on the blur of those two days of riding. My relationship with Swan seemed unaffected by my inherent part in the loss of his hand or the strange outburst of anger I had leveled at him, despite clearly grieving for his lost limb. I struggle even today with the difficulties he will face with a missing arm. But he would not wish those thoughts on me, I know. He remained friendly to me until the end. He was, as he had been since the hour we met, a celestially kind person.

Before I left his bedside for the last time, he grabbed my hand excitedly.

"One last thing, my friend," he said. "I have thought long and hard about what I want to tell you." He then paused for a second, his chin buried in his chest as if he were contemplating something. My hand was still held in his.

"People are . . . bad at saying goodbye," he continued, still staring fixedly at his feet at the end of the bed. He then let go of my hand, leaned over to the other side of his bed, and ripped off a small leaf from some flowers I had brought him that were sitting on his nightstand. It was a basket of violas, one of the only easy-to-find winter flowers.

Leaning back toward me, he brought his closed hand over and held it out. I raised my hand obediently to meet it. Grasping the back of my fingers, he pressed the leaf into my palm with his thumb and brought it level with our connected gaze. The veins of the leaf stood out in concordance with the ridges and lines of my skin.

"Flower Boy, you must look at the valleys and ask why."

With that, he gave me one last crescent moon grin, and we departed.

I experienced a profound feeling of understanding between the two of us after that, or at least, I felt that he understood me.

After it all, I left the West a cold, sad, and beaten traveler with only the memory of the *dúupuule* and a few scrambled notes for my troubles. What's more, these feeble triumphs were also only accomplished at the risk of Swan's life. Despite this, I was not nearly as distraught as I had been after my fruitless search for the stylite star, or even my solitary expedition to hunt for the orphan orchid. At first, I assumed this was because I had technically found the object of my search and was even able to view it up close, but I quickly came to realize that was not right. The difference was that this time, under the wild influence of instinct, I had managed to find something else: a friend.

Letter addressed to Marco Arwaldt from James Torrey
Gloucester, UK
December 17, 1832

Dear Marco,

Do you remember those winters back home? We wouldn't get
snow until January some years. Then it would come in a
flurry for a couple days before vanishing back into the
West over the river. This is not one of those years, and a
foot of snow has already covered the roof of the front
porch. I'm afraid most of the flowers at home died while I
was away, and I doubt I will have enough time to
recultivate until the final two steps in this journey are
complete. It is hard, truly, but almost all of my mother's
favorites just can't survive these early winters without
careful care. I couldn't even rush some inside to really
test your trick with the fruit bowl again. Out of the
garden, the only things not covered in snow were the
potted chrysanthemums that sat on the porch. I have moved
them inside, but they won't last through the week,
regardless of what room I put them in.

Needless to say, I'm home now, but I can't stay here
for long. It's difficult for me to explain. There is this
sort of driving, bubbling, wind-like thing inside . . .
well, never mind.

I arrived at my home to find your letter with my new
ticket and schedule, and I am ready to leave next month.
I'm sure the weather will hold out for us. After all, I
hear it barely snows in the city, even in season.

I am ready . . . I am. At least this one needs
little finding; Kew has done that work for us, and, after

all, you will be there with me this time. I'll see you in London, Marco.

    — J

6. The Crown of Spring Grass (*Poa primavera*)

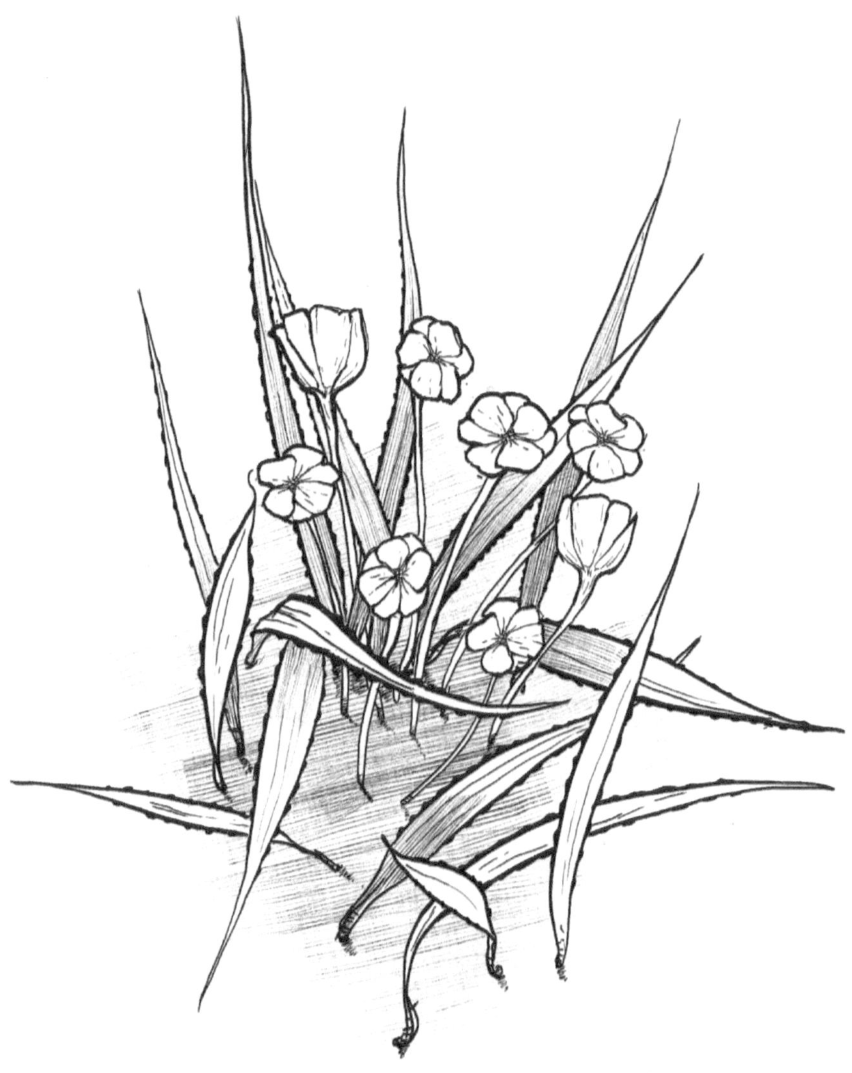

Location:

Poa primavera is extinct in the wild. While there have been reports of sightings and successful expeditions as late as 1820, all known naturally occurring specimens have died as of 1829. Previously, it was native to the rolling hills of northeastern Scotland, where it grew in many of the large grasslands of the country's northern peninsula. It flourishes in mildly wet soil, grows symbiotically with the common perennial ryegrass (*Lolium perenne*), and thrives in moderately warm and dry climates. While its most common bloom period is in the springtime, it has shown the ability to bloom much sooner, often as early as February, if adequately cared for.

Cultivation:

The rapid degradation of the plant's population has led to its careful cultivation in two major botanical gardens: the Kew Gardens in southwest England, and the Royal Botanical Gardens in Belfast, Scotland. The more prodigious of the two, the Royal Gardens, has had the plant in cultivation since the establishment's inception in 1828, while the Kew Gardens started its private cultivation in 1820. Since its insertion into scientific care, *Poa primavera* has been shown to display remarkable resilience when properly attended to, leading to the Kew Gardens releasing their blooms to national scientific observation once a year. Despite this, and due to an overabundance of caution regarding the species' welfare, the flowers are still exceedingly understudied and practically invisible to the general public.

Description:

The *P. primavera* grass shares a unified root system, causing instances of its growth to be classified as a single organism. A whole field of the grass, if such a growth existed, would be considered a single plant, though no growths exceeding three to four meters in width have ever been recorded.

The grass itself is similar in superficial appearance to the common sword grass, being hard and sharp to the touch due to silica deposits in its cell structures. The hollow blades are dark green, grow from the base root system upward, and extend up to a maximum height of thirty centimeters.

Despite its potential for immense size, each *P. primavera* organism only grows a single set of flowering blooms at one time. Each instance of the bloom manifests as a small ring of blossoms, containing anywhere from five to twenty small flowers called spikelets. This "crown" or bushel of flowers gives the plant its name and is where the grass receives most of its nutrients, both solar and otherwise—through the proprietary structure of its flowers.

The flowers are usually light yellow in color and bloom once a year, consistently opening for up to four months before wilting and dying. The flowers grow on thin, smooth stalks between the grass blades, as opposed to at the blades' apexes, and usually erupt within days of their adjacent sister growths. The external morphology of the plant is considerably complex, and the underlying processes that allow the plant to nurture its large amount of cellular mass with such a small bloom are still unknown.

Recovered entry from James Torrey's journal
Dated January 30, 1833

Marco, who has graciously agreed to accompany me on this trip, has asked me once more to shorten my personal notes on these expeditions. He fears that my work has become decreasingly scientific with each journey, and although I am much less concerned with this than he is at this point in my deliberations, I will again attempt to heed his friendly and amiable advice.

I know, really, that he hasn't told me everything the editors have sent back to him. This is not exactly some grand revelation. He has always been like that. I'm sure he fears that I will fall a little too far from what is acceptable and commit the horrible crime of submitting an article without a single centimeter range in it.

To be honest, I find that thought funny. What a ridiculous profession I find myself in. The interest and confusion showed by Anisa, Swan, even the mute cook aboard the St. Silas — their words often come back and swim through my head.

But there are more plans to be made. There are measurements to be taken and ships to board. That, at least, is a direction. I will respect my editor's opinion as much as I can and attempt to be brief when discussing my work while visiting the crown of spring. He is waiting for me this time. I can hardly wait.

Personal Notes:

During my expedition in America, Marco had stayed in London, taking care of a thesis he intended to finish by the end of the year. His usual vivacity for science and literature has also always been coupled with an overwhelming amount of caution, sometimes to an amusing extent. I remember him canceling a study trip we had planned during the break before our final spring term because the recorded average temperature of that spring was five degrees colder than the year previous. After confronting him about such a bizarre and frankly ridiculous decision, he adamantly told me that the breed of horses he had hired for our trip had a history of performing poorly in cold weather.

I invited him to accompany me on my previous two expeditions, but he sadly always replied with a polite denial. Of course, I never expected an answer in the affirmative, and knew the real reason for his denial was his aversive disposition, which bordered on fearfulness. These denials I accepted lightheartedly, and I started to ask almost as a joke, but this surprising acceptance I received with utter elation.

The trip we planned was to the Kew Gardens. Our intent was to catch the horse-drawn railway to Richmond from St. Flora the day after I arrived in England, and the trip was to last the blessedly short period of only three days. The domesticity and brevity of the journey were no doubt the deciding factors in my friend's diminished reluctance. Of course, I didn't really care what it took, and was just happy to see my friend again in person. His letters had been a lifeline for me during the previous three years, and a physical reunion would be a veritable rescue ship.

Marco sent me my visitation ticket by mail. It was wrapped in soft brown paper so as not to smudge the ink, and the large "PARTY SIZE: 2" stamped into the concluding bracket practically sent me over the ocean on its own.

*

The cart ride to Richmond was wonderfully smooth. Marco, wearing a soft brown suit and jacket, told me he felt very comfortable even though we were slightly exposed to the windy chill of the gently rolling English countryside.

"What a day . . . what a London day," he said quietly as our cart arrived. The cart's ceiling and side were almost completely made of thick glass windows that were framed in a charcoal wood, which allowed the riders to view the hills and skyline of the passing municipal neighborhoods and surrounding backcountry. The sky was brazen and bright, the clouds high and starch white.

We talked for almost the entire journey, a ride of almost two hours. I was mostly the originator of topics, Marco being a cool observer and sorter of my ideas in conversation and profession. It felt like we had never been apart.

"I should take more municipal journeys, if they are to be like this," I said as the ebbing macadam gave way to moss-covered cobblestone.

He relaxed back in answer, the sun glinting in his eyes with the smooth motion. A wider smile spread across his mouth as he regarded me out of the corner of his eye. A comfortable silence settled in, and we both turned our heads to watch the amber hills toddle past our window like infant sheep.

We arrived at the Kew Gardens on the second day, taking yet another cart from our small hotel room in Richmond. It was beautifully sunny, and the platinum clouds skipped by, aided in creating their passing sensation by the rush of the people around us. As we ventured deeper into the town, the sun shone slantways on the streets, reflecting off the steel rims of Marco's round glasses and the buttons of my traveling coat. He walked briskly beside me, clicking the heels of his shoes on the shining cobblestone walkway and leading me forward. We wound between street carts and crowds, passing so close to some people I thought we might bump their shoulders in passing. No collision ever occurred, however, and

I was left to hobble behind Marco, weaving in and out of sports coats and Sunday dresses in his wake.

As we rounded a rather thickly cluttered street corner, Marco suddenly stopped in front of me and put a hand out to his side. Barely stopping before running into him, I looked at him in confusion. The almost comical look on his face was one I had seen many times. It was the face he made when thinking hard about a certain subject that he just couldn't quite grasp. Slowly, he turned to his right, militarily pivoting on his heel. Following his eyes, I realized that the huge gates of the Kew Gardens lay in front of us, towering almost two stories above our heads. We had almost walked right past it.

"It's . . . incredible," I said.

Marco's eyebrows rose over his glasses and his chin jutted out slightly into a nod. "Indeed."

It was.

The tall gabled gate stretched skyward. Its black iron bars only minimally obscured the vivid green expanse behind it. One could see a decorative knot of creeping budless vines that clawed their way through the joints of the gate and curved around the adjacent brick wall. Behind the gate, stretching beyond the horizon of a gentle slope, lay a vibrant slice of what was to come. The grass was emerald and monochromatic. Daedalian curves of elaborate, flower-filled wood trellises, meters in length, bordered the massive walkway that connected to the gate. The whole effect was binary and striking, as if the gray of the city was magically banished or absorbed by the portal of the massive black egress. Our mesmerized state was broken only by the voice of a man calling Marco's name.

"Ah, Mr. Arwaldt! Right over here!"

The curator of the gardens was a short, stout man who looked like a plant himself. His brown suit flapped about his beltline in the gentle breeze, and the cuffs of his pants were just a little too big for his narrow ankles.

I shook his hand and was met with a smile and a pair of the most beautifully green eyes I had ever seen, like the leaves of a cherry tree in spring. They glistened in the sunlight, reflecting the white beams of the sun back at me.

"Come in, come in, gentlemen," he said, spreading his arms. "Welcome to the magnificent Kew Gardens!" He said it in a way that made me believe, if only for a second, that every time he walked into this palace of green, he too was seeing it for the first time.

The Gardens were alien in their beauty. Spanning almost seventy hectares, long stretches of sward stretched out over the perceptible hill of the plot. It was dotted by hulking, veined trees so thick and uniform that they looked like pillars of warm brown clay supporting a verdant ceiling of radiant dye. Set out in slanting rows were a number of small greenhouses liberated from the center of the establishment by an enormous, circular garden larger than any I had ever seen. Being stuck in the middle of the Gardens—walled in by a giant, vine-covered fence—created the most magical feeling of comforting isolation. The sounds of the surrounding city faded away, and it was as if I were no longer in Britain, but in my own imagination.

Flowers, expertly planted across wide swathes of land, formed diamonds and stars on the lawn. The slight upward tilt of the ground allowed one to view the patterns curated by the gardeners in a perfect, sloping picture. On the far side, barely seeable because it was shrouded in willow branches, was a tall brick building, almost church-like in its stateliness.

"What is that over there?" I asked, pointing toward it.

"That, my friend, is our botanical library," came the reply while the curator led us farther from the entrance and toward the first greenhouse. "Don't worry, we'll get to that. We'll get to everything in due time."

The various small greenhouses erected across the property were each set at slightly different humidities, lending themselves to the cultivation of their respective tropical and temperate flowers.

"Here are our beautiful *Liliums*. Ah, and here the fickle *Phalaenopsis*, incredibly difficult to grow in this weather, but we toil like it is our job."

The roads of the gardens were paved in cobblestone like the street outside but curved into thin diamonds and crosshatched walkways. In the middle of the central garden lay a massive fountain. It, like everything in the area, was surrounded by a ring of layered flowers. First red, then pink, purple, and finally yellow. They were placed expertly on terraced stone embankments in the shape of a massive and impossibly intricate pyramid. Marco, who had listened intensely as the curator explained the theories behind the structure of the garden, smiled a little at this gaudy font as we walked up to it.

"The fountain is a wonder of modern construction," explained the curator. "Beneath our feet lies a network of thin ducts, which are all shooting outward from this spot. The water from the fountain provides irrigation for almost 180 meters of cultivation space." He tapped his heel on the cobblestone as if he expected it to ring hollow. "Of course, we collect rainwater from the roofs of our many glasshouses, but most of the primary garden is adequately cared for by the fountain and the English rain. In contrast, it takes an average of five thousand liters of water a week to keep everything healthy inside the glasshouses. In particularly dry seasons, we have to mulch the soil of some of our rarer specimens to prevent evaporation, but that's all in a day's work."

*

Partially recovered entry from
James Torrey's journal
No date given

Oh, the Gardens.

I was in love. The whole area was magical in its enormity and peacefulness, and yet the courtyard we were exploring was only a fraction of the garden's total area. The fountain itself was chipped out of a massive slab of marble. Titanic in its presence, it had been made in the shape of a female gardener in a wide-brimmed evening hat, reaching up with a watering can toward the clouds as if collecting an invisible rain. This curved vessel served as the spout of the fountain, and a small, splayed lip of marble gave the water a fanned and arching trajectory. Her face was veiled in shadow from the sharp cut of the morning sun. She was clad in a long, flowing gardening frock that ended just above her ankles; the veins and cracks of the stone were blended artfully into each bend and fold of the dress. It had been cut to look like linen, with a sash of asymmetrical motion giving the appearance of a breeze blowing past her waist. Rounded marble ruts dropped themselves below her naked feet and led the streams of crystal-clear water into the underground irrigation ducts.

The flower-filled yard was ringed with tall trees, and I thought that they marked the limit of the premises, but this was not so. The cobblestone walkways pushed past these into concentrated forests of tree species, each separated by roads and cordoned off by thin black ropes. The light from the sun shimmered as it poked through the twinkling leaves of the canopy, kaleidoscoping its way through the roof of limbs.

The whole morning I was gripped by a desire to work in this Edenic paradise, but quickly accepted the impossibility of such a commitment. Not only did I lack the qualifications, but foregoing America altogether would probably be too much for me. So, instead of indulging in that specific daydream, I basked in the area's brilliance as a visitor, and thoroughly convinced myself that this had its merits too. With only a slight twist of perspective, I comforted myself with the idea that the magic of the place would last longer in my memory than it would have in the experience of a prolonged stay.

We entered the greenhouse nearest the fountain. It was made of rippled glass, minted together into massive, uninterrupted sheets of crystal. The walls and ceiling were all gilded in this thick material, and the light shone unimpeded, flooding the room with reflections of red and green and violet. Pots hung from every side, encasing the place in a hedge-like magic: a maze of flowers, fungi, and color. I had to stop myself from just running end to end, looking at each flower and leaf in the building and endlessly breathing in the pollenated air. The heat from the sun hung low and damp, and mists of perspiration shimmered upward from the ground. I have never seen such a place in my life, and I doubt that I ever will again. It was exquisitely, magically beautiful.

Finally, the whole experience was capped with an exploratory visit to the library. Its shelves stood two men tall on both the first and second floor. Thin rolling ladders splayed out over the vestibules. Their ends connected to running tracks on the floor and the tops of the shelves; this allowed them to run freely along the rows. The second floor was composed of a ring of walkways that left the center of the building open. Low, carved railings allowed librarians and clients to look over the edge from above and view the first floor like perched owls. Marco spent a good hour there, walking from shelf to shelf in the funny, wooden way he does when he gets excited. I remember his astonishment at beholding a rotary book holder that allowed an absorbed librarian to have up to six books open at once for comparative study, all easily available at the touch of a hand.

I admit, I also fell to romantic thoughts here. Near the end of the tour, I left our guide and Marco. Searching through the library, I realized that the shelves were organized by author names, in alphabetical order — quite different from the fixed location style of organization that was used in school. With timid delight, I grazed the books' spines, gliding past shelf after shelf before finally reaching a dimly lit corner near the back. Reaching up, I slid my finger between "A Study of Archaic Flower Worship" by Alexander Torque and "The Cultivation: A Clarifying Appeal to Modern Botany" by Michelle Torstar, making a small gap just large enough for another book to fit.

*

After about four hours—during which the curator showed us through almost the entirety of the main garden surrounding the fountain, five whole greenhouses (each equally majestic and individual), and the aforementioned library—we reached a small shady corner of the plantation. Thrushes and goldfinches glided between us and the sun. At the edge of a narrow cobblestone walkway, there lay a tiny pond nestled against the wall of the sanctuary. Before us stood the object of my search.

I almost missed it and would have walked by obliviously had the curator not stopped and pointed it out. Marco had told the man what I was in need of seeing, and he seemed just as excited to show it off as we were to observe it.

"The jewel of the sanctuary!" he announced, spreading his arms wide to gesture at the ground. "The crown of spring: the *Poa primavera.*"

I had previously only seen the name in writing, and having an expert say the name aloud materialized and solidified the object into reality while simultaneously adding to its strange kind of tactile mythicality. The grass was exquisitely sharp-looking and thick, like a hundred daggers poking up from the ground. I stood avidly at the clearing's edge, getting a closer look. The blades were not only hard and long, but almost half an inch thick, an attribute that alluded to their hollow core. Touching one of the closest ones lightly on the side alerted me to how sharp the silica made them; the material added to the already visually striking blade-like quality.

"May I show you something, Mr. Torrey?" the curator said, kneeling before the edge of the grass next to where I stood. I consented and attempted to kneel next to him.

"No, no, sir, I'll have you standing for this if you don't mind."

I stood back up.

"Look there," he said, stretching his hand out over the grass blades' sharp, rippled tips. "Do you see that dark patch just there? It is easier to see from above."

I focused on the spot he indicated and felt Marco's face tilt slowly forward at my side as he too examined the spot. He squinted through his glasses. Slowly, as my eyes defocused, a slight ovaloid outline materialized. It wasn't so much an indentation as it was a color shift. The bright emerald shine of the grass darkened to a deeper, sea green. The center of the oval also had blades with noticeably ill-defined edges, as if they had been rounded off by sandpaper.

Marco put his hand on my shoulder, smiling, and pointed to another spot. This time, he gently guided me to a patch about a foot to the left. Another darkened spot shone obliquely near the first. I looked again, closely this time, and saw that this patch of grass was also slightly lower than its surroundings.

"A footprint," Marco said, almost in a whisper.

"You are very observant, my friend," cheered the man, practically clapping his hands together in excitement at Marco's gesture. "The *primavera* grass has the remarkable ability to heal its grass blades, even if they are severely damaged, provided that the central ring of flowers remains unharmed. It can often recover blades of grass in as little as three days after an injury. It is an incredibly—and beautifully—resilient organism."

"That," said Marco, smiling, "is not in the textbooks."

"Quite true, quite true," replied the curator, lifting his eyebrows and smiling. "Printing and publishing are slow processes, are they not? But that is why you are here, Mr. Torrey, in front of the thing itself instead of off in some archive somewhere."

"Yes," I murmured back, still squinting at the darkened spot on the ground.

"Unfortunately, due to this ability, many . . . exuberant individuals visit our exhibition with the intention of damaging it to see if the claims are indeed true. That patch right there was made by a malcontent's foot no more than four days ago! Just look how uniformly it grows now. Beautiful . . . no, powerful, isn't it? Now, to the flowers. After all, that is your specialty, right Mr. Torrey?"

I was in awe, but quickly recovered as the curator left the walkway, motioning us to follow. He led us around the grass patch and onto another walkway made of marble steppingstones. Letting me pass him, he indicated with an open hand a set of identical stones laid in the grass that led straight up to the middle of the proprietary clearing. Stepping onto these carefully, I was able to get a close look into the middle of the grass patch.

The flowers, of which there were only six, were a pasty, soft yellow and had a texture almost like the outer shell of an insect. They were even a little translucent, and at certain angles, I could see the light of the sun bouncing off the pond water and through the petals. The centers of the flowers were a darker mustard yellow, save for one, which I noticed was slightly paler than the others. This discoloration intrigued me, but I could not quite reach it from the vantage point of the last stable stone. I was so close, barely a stride away. I turned back to them, but before I could ask, Marco had already seen what I wanted.

"Would he be able to get any closer, Doctor?" he said, inclining his neck down to address him.

"I'm afraid not, gentlemen. Even though the grass itself is particularly resilient, the flowers do not share that attribute. Do you see that one flower in the circle, the lighter colored one? That is the flower that contains the stamen and is the most fragile part of the plant. It is, unfortunately, not something we can have people touching or getting close to, as such activities might put the integrity of our cultivation at risk. I'm sure you understand."

The whole area started to swim in front of me as he ended his declination. The flower in question reminded me of the amber grain seeds of America, and for a sad, solitary moment, I was transported back to the uncharted West, wrestling a horse through the marshy wetland of the dead prairie. I almost fell too far into my imagination, my mind creating more and more of the environment as I stood spellbound. I felt for a moment like I was going to fall into a reverie or faint, but just as I felt the deepest wave of emotion well up, I was rescued by Marco's hand once more at my shoulder.

"You're alright, James," he said in my ear. He must have walked quickly onto the stones behind me. "They are definitely spikelets, aren't they? I was expecting them to be more like the flowers of the *Sisyrinchium,* those evening grasses we studied second year, but they are not even close. How interesting."

And I was ripped completely back into the thrushed Eden of the Kew Gardens and the wide, palatial walls of gray England.

*

It was close to dusk now, and the evening had been a wonderful success. I decided to walk back to the hotel instead of taking the carriage. Marco had said he had business to attend to somewhere else in the city and expressed a need to take the ride, so I told him to go on ahead and that I would meet him at our hotel room later. He begrudgingly agreed and left me with a map marked with the path back to our lodging.

The day had at least four hours left in it, and I strolled merrily through the narrow streets and alleyways of the city as it wound itself down. The gentle clanking sound of horse carriages carried me past uncountable rows of English shops, some even with flower baskets hanging from their signposts. I was surprised at the way I enjoyed the domestic brick of the city almost as much as the natural beauty of the meadow, and my mesmerized state carried me along once again. The shops and bustle of other people crafted an atmosphere so different from the one I had grown up with in the rural country of Tennessee.

Before I knew it, I had walked almost three quarters of the way back. I felt tired and stopped at a park bench to take a break. After looking around and taking in every detail of the passersby and their homes, my head dipped a little, and I found myself looking at a crack in the worn macadam dirt between my feet. The crack wound its way toward me from the road gutter and widened a little as it crept under the toe of my shoe. I noticed a tiny flower sprouting through the crack at its terminus, barely two centimeters from where my foot had stopped as I sat down. Had I moved my foot even a little bit over in my rest, I would have surely crushed it into nothing. As luck would have it, I had not done so, and just like every English bench-sitter before me, I had spared the life of the tiny plant.

My eyes focused on the flower, fighting its way up through the layered effort of humanity. It had a bright set of rounded white petals, and a common yellow center of carpels. I recognized it almost at once as a member of the *Ranunculus* family: a tiny pale buttercup growing in the brown and gray human jungle.

A distant memory suddenly resurfaced in my head. It was an image of my old botany teacher at college. He had mentioned the *Ranunculus* many times in his lectures, mostly to the chagrin of his bored students who had come to study complex botanical chemistry. The man would go on and on, relating the buttercup and various other plants of his liking to stories, telling us of the wonders of the Latin names, the rituals of past societies, and the flower games of ancient English and Bohemian children.

"The buttercup is a fascinating creature, nominally and botanically," I remember him saying while staring off into the corner of the room; he was completely lost within his own world. "The Latin name *Ranunculus* is the diminutive of *Rana*, the word for frog or toad. *Ranunculus* in English would be 'little toad,' or the more accurate and pleasurable translation, 'wee little toad.' The English name 'buttercup' was given to the plant because it was believed that the yellow pigment turned cow's milk yellow when it was made into butter if the animal in question had consumed the flower before being milked. This, of course, is ridiculous and untrue. In fact, buttercups are poisonous to bovines."

Unhindered by the impatient groans of the class, he went on. "German children used to put buttercups under their chins. If the yellow hue was reflective, then the child was said to have a fondness for butter. How that started I haven't the slightest. And yet in Greece, before the Germans' time, escaped slaves used to rub the pollen of the little frog on their tattoo brands to erase the marks of their previous owners. In America, the Nez Perce call it *iceyéeyenm sílu*, the 'coyote's eye.' These Native Americans believe that the coyote got his eyes stolen by the vicious eagle and fashioned new ones out of the buttercups growing nearby. Hardly a name deserving of a diminutive, wouldn't you say?"

The church bell outside rang past the hour, but his tangential train of thought still ran on for five or more minutes. I remember Marco stayed in his seat past even the teacher's dismissal, furiously scribbling notes.

After a moment or two more in the memory, I reached into my pants pocket and took out my stamped visitation ticket, still wrapped in its brown parchment from when Marco had sent it in the mail. After finding a pencil in the chest pocket of my coat while I held the parcel in between my fingers, I unfolded the parchment and started writing on it.

7. The Buttercup (*Ranunculus fallax*)

Location:

Primarily a European plant, *Ranunculus* has spread easily through the northern part of America. It can be found in poorly drained areas that include, but are not limited to, prairies, meadows, grazing pastures, swamps, gardens, bogs, clay deposits, and gravel pits. This wide variety of possible growing environments shows a remarkable resiliency and growing plasticity. Though it is rarely found in dry grassy areas, some variant species can grow in such conditions as well. It is definitively perennial and has no specific blooming season. The flower is herbaceous and can be both aquatic, and/or terrestrial. Specimens grow easily in many varied environments around the world.

Cultivation:

Due to its ravenous growing ability, *Ranunculus* is considered a weed by the majority of people in the botanical and gardening communities. Its easy growth around other plants can disturb delicate root structures and crowd other, more desired species. It can also negatively influence the grazing of nearby livestock due to its toxicity. Despite this, the plant is still occasionally used as a decorative flower and is usually planted around the exterior of well-insulated gardens as an ornamental blossom. Its toxic oil has been used homeopathically in the treatment of rheumatism and headaches, though the efficacy of this medical practice is questionable and is still being researched.

Description:

The leaves are almost always bright green and appear solely as a rosette at the base of the stem. The flower usually displays a small five-petal bloom that is cup-shaped and shaded yellow, green, or white. Each petal has a corresponding nectar gland at its base. The petals are unusually reflective and at times mirror-like, especially in yellow-colored species. This serves to regulate heat as well as attract pollinators due to its bright reflection of the sun's light during the day. Its central anthers are usually arranged in a spiral helix and can be white or yellow. The small fruits, or achenes, of the flower can be smooth, hairy, winged, knobby, or spinal. The flower primarily reproduces through long running structures called stolons, which grow out from originator flowers to form new ones, although the presence of the achenes confirms its ability to reproduce through seeds as well. The flower is toxic to both humans and animals, containing a harsh, bitter protoanemonin oil that causes blistering in the mouth and throat if ingested. The oil itself originates as a purer form of the chemical, which breaks down under pressure to form the final toxin. Interestingly enough, though most cattle avoid the plant due to its horribly bitter taste, the oil has also been shown to have addictive qualities. In rare cases, cattle have been observed to eat the flower until it kills them due to internal hemorrhaging. The oil is denatured after drying, allowing buttercup-ridden hay to still be safely used as feed.

*

Letter addressed to Mr. Marco Arwaldt from Denis Laurent,

Editor in Chief of "Journal Des Savants"

Gloucester, UK

February 1, 1833

Response to Consultant's Application for Publication

Publication: Flowers of the Far Fields

Author(s): James Torrey

Field: Botany

Language: English

Status: Rejected

Grounds for Rejection: Inconsistent tone, lack of citations, lack of cohesive scientific style elements, improper coinage.

Additional Notes: Not applicable

It was almost eight o'clock when I arrived back at my hotel. The sun had already set, settling like fire-melted butter behind the soft square outlines of Richmond's business district. If one looked carefully, they could see the outline of the black creeper vines climbing up the westward side of the borough's lone cathedral, which faced the winding and unpredictable Thames.

I walked up the spiral staircase of our hotel, making sure to move across the thinly carpeted floor so as not to disturb our neighbors. I inserted my key in the lock and slipped inside, turning around and closing the door as carefully as I could.

"James," came Marco's voice from behind me. I turned around. Something about the tone alerted me. It was ever so slightly softer than usual. Marco always talked with clean, perfect diction, like he was in court.

He stood at the end of our unlit room; a letter clutched in his hands. He wore a painted smile. I strolled over to the couch near the entrance and sat down, regarding him as I took off my hat and gloves.

"Another denial?"

He looked up from the letter, an expression of surprise on his face. Recovering, he blinked at me. "I'm afraid so," he said. "I was unaware that . . . well, that you were aware of the others after the first."

I smiled back. "I suspected."

He nodded in response, his eyes drifting back down to the letter.

"What was it for this time?"

"Coinage," Marco said, turning slightly so as to regard me over the top of the paper, the note obscuring the beginnings of a frown.

I shrugged.

He set the paper down, the mask disappearing slowly to reveal a somber look. "I'm afraid this is not the only letter we have received." As he said this, he pulled out another note from his vest pocket. It was cut with a letter opener and the contents were thick and bulging. The glint of a scarlet seal shone off the front like a badge. The paper silently unfolded from his hand. Marco twirled the letter around in his fingers. The beveled wax took the shape of the Dresden University crest.

"I've been accepted," he said, and left it at that.

Letter addressed to James Torrey from Marco Arwaldt

Black Hawk, TN, USA

April 1, 1833

Dear James,

It pains me a great deal to write this . . . and after everything: all except the last flower. My resources, though not entirely used up, have come back dry in the last couple of weeks. I even sent a letter to my friend Francis Beaulieu, the port master of the closest port to Mauritius I could find, but he has yet to answer me. I am again writing this in haste, this time just before leaving to fill my new position at Dresden.

It appears that I will fail to provide you with adequate accommodations in the time I have. I would tell you that I could continue my search once I get to my destination, but I cannot lie to you, James. In fact, I fear my occupational duties have already eclipsed the allotted time I have given them, and I know now that I will need to dedicate much more of my energy to this new position than I had previously thought.

I will have to leave you; or rather, I will need to leave this last leg to you, and all I can ask for is your forgiveness.

I have sent four more possible contacts to you attached to this letter: the remnants of the portfolio I had previously dedicated to this trip. They are each captains of individual ships that are bound for your destination by the end of the season, and one should almost assuredly be able to give you passage.

Please, above all else, make sure you are safe. We have been lucky previously, and you have admirably kept yourself out of danger despite the terrible fates that have swirled around you. I could not forgive myself if you were taken away on this last trip.

Protect yourself, even if it means leaving the flower behind. There are, in the end, things more important than a publication promise.

Yours,

Marco

Letter addressed to Marco Arwaldt from James Torrey
Gloucester, UK
June 9, 1833

My dear friend, thank you.
There is so much I would like to say, but I haven't the
words. My book, my flowers, my friends, even my mother's
garden would not be the same without your help, and I
struggle to imagine how horrid an undertaking this would
have been without you by me. In a way, this manuscript is
more yours than mine. I cannot thank you enough.

You should not worry. After all, I have learned from
the best how to plan and execute such trips as this, and
one more voyage is within my power. I promise that. I will
make it back.

I have just written to two of the merchant ships you
mentioned. I should be able to send you a letter before
leaving notifying you of my vessel and sail dates. That
will hopefully put your heart at ease. Ships don't sink
these days, anyway. My travels and our letters have at
least taught me that.

My provision fund has started to run thin now that I
near the end, but I know it will be enough. After all,
what did we expect in the end? Everything to be perfect?
I choose to remember otherwise. The crushing walls of
disappointment have a habit of affecting history like
that.

Please, write to me about Dresden. It will be
something for me to look forward to upon my return. I want
to hear it all.

Letter addressed to Marco Arwaldt from James Torrey
Dresden University, Germany: Mailbox 24
August 13, 1833

September 1: New York, The Aurelia. One way to Mauritius.

It is done. I'm off one last time. I will send you word when I return. I only wish I could give you an address as a kindness, but I do not have one for you. I will check the port office as often as I can for letters, but please do not feel pressured to send one there. I don't even have a return date for you, but I will make sure to write to you once I'm back in Black Hawk. Just one more, Marco. One more left.

— J

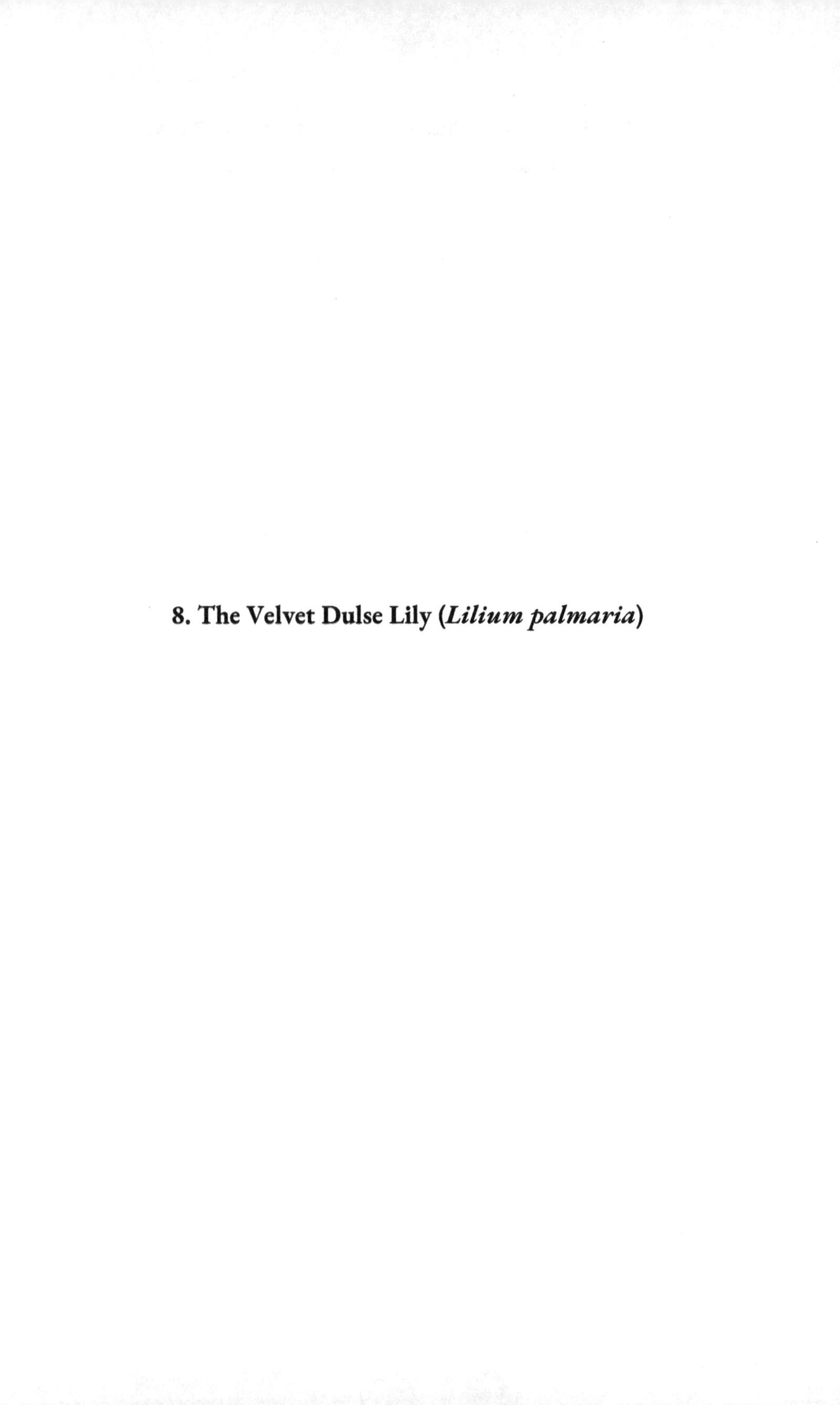

8. The Velvet Dulse Lily (*Lilium palmaria*)

Location:

Lilium palmaria has only been observed in the shallow waters off the eastern coast of Mauritius, about 1,500 kilometers east of the island of Madagascar, and reportedly blooms only once every five years. Though lilies are usually impossible to grow in saline environments, let alone submerged ones, *L. palmaria* is endemic to the sand beds of the island's beaches and lives its entire life under water. The survival of the plant is thought to be due to its peculiar symbiotic relationship with the native red dulse seaweed. The spores of the seaweed attach to the seed of the lily during the initial phase of growth and protect it from the otherwise fatal effect of the surrounding seawater. This allows the plant to bloom and gives it its characteristic deep red hue. This protection's underlying processes are still unknown, and the paradoxical nature of the plant adds to its mythical status in the modern botanical collective mind. To date, many questions are still asked about the nature of the algae–flora relationship, including where the flower obtains nutrients, how it reproduces, whether its relationship to the dulse is parasitic or purely symbiotic, and why a flower bloom is biologically necessary in an aquatic environment. It should be stated that before this expedition, no scholarly documentation has yet been published positively classifying the species, and belief in its extant nature is based on the adamant hearsay and personal accounts of the island's occupants.

Cultivation:

There is currently no known way to successfully cultivate *Lilium palmaria*. This impossibility is due to its reliance on the dulse seaweed and its defiance of observation in nature. To date, only one documented attempt to find and harvest the flower has been made by the Laurey Botanical Institute in England. This ended in failure after the researchers were unable to locate the flower after several weeks of investigation.

The expedition was a purely conjectural venture by the institute and has not been replicated by any other person, university, or botanical organization.

Description:

Lilium palmaria is a flowering aquatic plant which grows from bulbs, similar to its cousin of the Lilieae tribe, *Notholirion* (the terrestrial Asian lily). It is thought to bloom about once every five years, depending on specific temperature and lighting conditions. The flower is almost always reported as a deep shade of velvet red, sometimes so dark as to appear black, although its rare bloom and dark ecosystem make adequately observing and classifying its color difficult. Structurally, the deep black or red petals are basal and curve backward toward its short stem, which is a similar structure to other *Lilium* variants such as the *LL. pumilum* and *davidii*. Additionally, descriptions report that its peculiar aquatic nature causes it to develop a more "cupped" appearance, similar to the Japanese *Lilium maculatum*. It is bulbous, short-stemmed, and grows to a maximum height of about ten centimeters. Long, tuberous growths of seaweed are commonly reported to grow "out" of the plant, but these reports are more than likely mistaken and based on growth of the separate algae organism; these segments should not be considered part of the *L. palmaria*'s structure.

*

Recovered entry from James Torrey's journal
No date given

This was it. What a wonderful and horrible experience this pursuit has become. I can barely write down the ending to the adventure which has consumed the last three years of my life. I fear that my work, this book of botany, will crumble into a personal narrative, and all my scientific credibility will be lost; but again, I cannot censor out the weight of this pursuit. Besides, perhaps this short text has already become more about me than my flowers.

I will quickly sum up the last year. In late July I started my preparation. I wanted nothing more than to rush off to Mauritius, but there was too much to do back home in America. That spring brought a mountain of paperwork that needed to be done. Since Marco could no longer organize the trips for me, I needed to hire a new editor or step up to the task. I chose the latter option, finding myself unable to bring another person on board so late in the project. Alone, I booked the ships, researched the previous attempt at locating the flower by the Laurey Institute, gathered what funds I had left, and got in touch by letter with my contacts at the port. I was in the preliminary planning period and still finishing up my writing on the previous entry when Marco's final letter of resignation came in. I was caught up in anxiety and distress and ceased all of my work for some time at that point, finding myself more than a little overwhelmed; but after the third day of lethargy, I got word that Marco had sent me another letter, and I picked it up at the post office as fast as I could.

This second letter was from Dresden, and it told me that Marco had been placed in the position of head botanical librarian, a career that would easily set him up for the rest of his life. Such an offer could not be refused. While we vaguely entertained ideas of him continuing to receive my drafts as a friend rather than an editor, we both knew such optimism was unfounded. Marco was just too busy. A frustration at my own reliance on his help bubbled up, and the letter lay on my desk for another day before I calmed down.

I sent him the plans. Like it or not, my journey was now solely my responsibility, and an eventual tide of confidence soon overpowered any feeling of embarrassment that had risen to the surface of my countenance initially.

He stated in the short letter that these past few years had been the best he could have hoped for, but that it was now time to part ways: me for my flowers, and him for his books. He left a university mailing address at the bottom.

This trip. I knew, would be difficult. I had been alone in America for some time, but Marco had always been at my metaphorical side in the East, and his professional absence threw me further into myself. I now believe that this was because my book, now ripped from its editor and cohort, was unequivocally, horribly mine. There was no one else to divide responsibility for this precarious ideal at its climax, and if it failed, which I fear it has, the weight of that foundering rested on

my shoulders and no one else's. If my writing cannot
live up to these experiences, then I have only my
flowers for editors, and I pray that will be enough.
Mistakes and all.

*

Preparation took the full month of August. I
planned on needing a boat, a captain, and enough money
to spend at least a month in the country. Though my
grant money ran out about three months before my planned
departure, I had saved enough from my tenure in America
to take care of most of my needs. This was made easier
by me being alone, but only monetarily. I told myself
that if I went broke on the island, then at least I
would have plenty of time to find the dulse lily, and
perhaps I could pay my dues with the money from this
book, if it was to make any at all.

Finally, at the start of September, after a long
period of agonizing stagnation filled with misery and
anxiety, I departed.

I boarded a large Indiaman in New York, and though
the weather was cold in America, I was assured by letter
from my hired navigator that my destination would be
warm enough. I packed lightly, bringing only two books
(one on Lilium and one on algae) for field reference.

*

The captain's name was Grisha Arthur. His ship was
named The Aurelia, and I remember my initial surprise
upon first setting eyes on the boat and her crew. While
nothing was broken or mishandled that I could tell, the
whole vessel seemed overladen with a white kind of rust,
including its seamen. Their beards and fingers were all

slightly off color, as if being so near the sea made the men fishlike and slippery. This grayish scaling of the wood and metal fixings was unnerving, and completely unlike the polish of the well-maintained fittings on the vessels I was used to, but I tried not to let it break my concentration. I would be in the warm climate of the Southern Sea soon, I thought. My last and most elusive prey would be found, and my story would be complete.

How wrong I was. My immaculately crafted timetable might as well have been thrown into the waves of the Vineyard Sound before we left for all the good it did me. It became apparent to me soon that the cargo ship was headed not to Mauritius, but to Australia first, and all the way south to Melbourne at that!

I remember being so angry at my captain's dishonesty that I stormed all the way through the main deck, up past the mainmast, and straight into the captain's quarters. In a tide of uncharacteristic frustration, I exploded at him, asking why he had not told me about this egregious detour during our correspondence beforehand.

Captain Arthur was less than sympathetic to my plight and talked in his usual grunting drawl, only saying, "We'll get us back. Pay no mind." He only repeated this afterward, increasing the intervals between the words to add emphasis when I pressed further. "Pay . . . no . . . mind."

I only remember clenching my fists and slamming the door as I left, back to my closet of a room.

*

The Aurelia quickly became my prison. At night, the shallow light of my lantern was easily smothered by the cold blackness of the waves in every direction. The atmosphere of brine seeped through the wooden ship and salted my teeth and nose. The slop of the waves mere centimeters away from my spinning head doled out a sickening metronomic time, making sure I was aware of every second that staggered by.

The days were only worse. While the sun shone bright for the first few weeks, the cold quickly crept out of the ocean current and into the crew's quarters where I slept. Eventually, even the sun was hidden behind the encumbering fog of the southern autumn. As we entered the South Atlantic Current, some bindings snapped near the ratlines due to the cold and needed to be repaired by the ship's carpenter. The passengers of the ship were forbidden to go aftward on deck or past the mainmast below, as those upper and lower decks belonged to the crew. Even if I had been allowed to travel past the front deck, I would not have had the courage to do so. The sailors, salt-crusted as they were, were all hard, scarecrow-like men who disliked conversation and travelers almost as much as they disliked their own line of work. Shouts and curses from drunken fights and gambling games could be heard echoing through the hollow craft throughout the night, putting even more obstacles in the way of blissful sleep. I remember the laughter around the card games the men played on the St. Silas, but those had been surrounded by mirth and heat. Whatever contests were taking place on the aft side of the ship, they were all accompanied by hateful hollers and the sounds of glass shattering.

Somewhat luckily, the omnipresent chill of the southwestern current foretold strong winds; I heard the captain, addressing the crew, assure them the trip to Australia would only take eighty days at most, putting us in Mauritius sometime in late November or Early December.

I admit, I cried silently in my hammock that night like I did in Asia. The knowledge of a timeline was, at first, a relief, but that relief brought with it a crushing resignation. My spirit for the expedition had already almost frozen over. Isolated in my dark room with my shallow hammock, those remaining months seemed like an uncrossable chasm of time. I was lucky that I brought those two books with me. They were undoubtedly my saving grace in that pit. As dry reading as they were, one of the only things that kept me from throwing myself off the top mast were the crude but beautiful orange renditions of the Japanese bell lilies. I remember imagining them covered in the velvet dulse weed, changing them into the object of this last adventure so far away. I was not even comforted by the grand port at Melbourne, for we stayed there only a day and were too soon off again on the wretched waves.

Because of this trip (which did not end until the eternity between our departure and the day of December 3 had crawled past), I no longer saw the sea as a shining baby blue like I once did in Asia and America, but as a cold, inexorable, sable black.

Personal Notes:

I bring you now to the final destination. I stumbled off that ship and onto the warm, welcoming sand of the island, my luggage tumbling behind me in a heap. I did not want to wait and see what the crew or captain planned to do during their stay, and instead walked straight out of the harbor and into the town. Mauritius is a warm island about two thousand kilometers east of Madagascar. The climate was nothing like I had ever experienced, and the crushing cold of the southern current slowly evaporated in the equator's heat. Here I procured a room for the month, and food was available at a town called St. Louis, only about a day's walk from my rented hut. The lily, I knew, was more likely to grow in the deeper parts of the reefs surrounding the eastern side of the island, and I spent my time during the first week and a half getting my bearings. Gradually, I started to recognize the landmarks that made up the shape and relief of the southeastern shoreline.

Even if I did find the plant, it was possible that it wouldn't be in bloom (as it flowered only about once every five years), but I had done my research, and each publication which mentioned its existence had noted that it was more likely to bloom in the time period I had chosen for my search. I was about two months late due to my captain's indifference, but I thought that should not matter too much, after all. The duty now lay in finding the flower somewhere under the lapping surf that crept back and forth over the pale beaches.

Thankfully, very few events occurred outside of my preparations after landing. My money, though slim, was not strained enough to worry me anymore. My frequent excursions into the shallows of the sea were fruitful in that they taught me a great deal about the shape of my surroundings. I could see that the island was vaguely pentagon-shaped, with its fifth point stretching northward toward the eastern tip of Africa. What I could not find out by observation, I discovered by talking to the locals, most of whom knew English and French. They warned me mainly of the dangerous fish in the area and of the unpredictable tides. I realized at that point that my experience with dangerous sea life was small and made a note in my journal to remedy this with whichever boatman I chose to take me out past the shallows.

The flower, if it could be found, would be on the south or southeastern side, I was sure. The point where the two sides met had a long peninsula that dropped almost instantly into a deep trench on either side, and it was there where I decided to start digging.

I say digging because I was doing just that; the delicate seaweed could have incredibly small stalks that required excavation. In order to narrow down my search from about ninety kilometers of coastline, I needed to find concentrations of the dulse, the red seaweed of the Indian and Atlantic Oceans. I first found it just north of the connecting peninsula. The sand, which I had been digging into with my hands a little ways off the shore, came up the color of wine as I dredged it over. The seaweed itself was a sight to behold. Its bottomless, almost purple redness stained the water and rocks with its hue, and I understood why it was a popular delicacy in the Atlantic. Even the monks of yesteryear were known to dry and eat the dulse during summer. I frantically dug up more and more and hauled it back to my hut to cook. The taste was savory and mellow, and I sat for almost half an hour watching it curl and wrinkle as it dried out on the fire. Even after the sea left the leaves, the depth of the velvet color persevered.

Eventually, I placed the roasting sticks in the sand a foot or so away from the flame so I could continue to admire the leaves' pigment without burning them. The seaweed alone did not provide me with much nourishment, but I went to bed content with the day's work. As I lay in the small wooden cot in my shack, I tried in my mind to twist and transmogrify the wrinkled weeds into the smooth, arching petals of a lily bloom. I ebbed into a gentle unconsciousness to the slow rhythm of the nearby tide and the much more distant sound of the Indian Ocean's crashing waves.

Then the fateful day.

The waves which had so completely defined my hell on *The Aurelia* woke me early on a cloudless morning almost two weeks after my arrival. I had already explored the entirety of the southeastern shoreline as well as the accompanying side of the island's peninsula in following the trails of the red dulse. Since that was done, it was time to progress further north, into the deeper ridges of the aquatic sand beds just past the shallows, a perfect spot for the flower.

My boatman, a man by the name of René Glory, woke early to meet me, and we pushed off into the water mere moments before the sun rose over the horizon. He was a taller man who had an almost emotionless face, not blank, but listless and accepting. He had wanted to leave in the afternoon for some reason I could not understand. My French was not particularly good, and he did not speak English, but I assured him to the best of my ability that I wanted to start in the brightest time of the morning to give myself the maximum amount of daylight. The seawater was clear in Mauritius, but as the seafloor slowly fell off into the oblivion of the deep, the radiance quickly disappeared, and there being no way to bring a light with me during my short diving excursions in likely places, the sun's particular angle of progress through the sky was my only hope of further exploration. He eventually accepted the money I offered timidly, and our deal was set.

It took us an hour to creep past the peninsula and into the northeastern side of the island. I spent the time directing René where to go, pushing him closer to the shore or farther away depending on the light and the presence of the dulse seaweed. The beach run-off divided itself into many inlets and aquatic valleys. I wanted to explore every one of them out to its furthest visible appendage.

I wore a dark leather suit I had brought from England to keep me warm while coming in and out of the water, but it was mostly unneeded. The water was incredibly warm, as was the air. It seemed I had left the cold fingers of the sea and now waded excitedly in its feverish breath.

After about three more hours, the sun was at the perfect angle to view the declining seabed farther out, and I began to grow anxious with anticipation. We had gotten about 50 meters from the shoreline when I discovered the existence of a sandbar about a ship's length from the boat. Excited by this, I gestured to René to pull straight along it as slow as he could.

This time, however, René refused with a quaver in his soft voice, and as I looked at him, his eyes were wide and seemed scared. So different from his original banal expression, his brow was knitted in a tight furrow, and his chin was bumpier than usual. A small amount of fear crept over me, and I looked back toward the seafloor I had been pointing to.

The waves had picked up slightly due to the wind coming from the west, but the draft was warm and slow. Gradually, my fears calmed again. I was fully prepared. I had planned this through and through, and nothing was going to stop me from exploring every inch of this island, especially not the facial expression of a boat guide.

I walked over to the other side of the skimmer and handed him a generous number of coins I had stashed in my wadded-up clothes. Such an offer might cost me a little down the road, especially on the way back home, but I was not worried about it at the time. All I could imagine was the sandbar rising steadily above a blanket of velvet lilies, and the sun slowly starting its declining dip westward.

René said something in French that I was unfamiliar with, but his eyes never left the money. I silently laid it on his lap and turned my back on the driver. I felt tense from the proximity of the flower. It was close. I could feel it, and this tenseness, I presume, is what caused my almost cold relationship with René in those moments. It was the fact that I needed him. His help, even past our incompatible language, was the final piece. I couldn't afford to take no for an answer.

I adamantly continued my observation over the bow to reinforce my gesture of perseverance, and, after a moment, the boat started gliding slowly forward again. After I sat back down, I peered more over the boat than I had before, my nose almost dipping into the water. I had to make sure I did not touch the surface, for the clear picture of the seafloor would be obscured—even more than it already was by the lapping waves. As we passed the edge of the bar, the water became almost magically clear and calm. With a widened eye I spied a long tendril of dulse seaweed spiraling up from a small, veiled point at its base on the seafloor, so black that it appeared to create a fathomless hole in the darkening sand. Eagerly I leaned forward further, shouting to René to nudge the boat a little closer toward the twisting aquatic bract.

Completely focused on the dulse, I blinked in surprise as I witnessed it slowly drift away. Without looking up, I yelled a little angrily at René to keep our course true and straight. He yelled my name back, much louder than I had expected. I pressed my palm onto the bow to push myself up and look back, when the boat gave a massive starboard lurch. I caught myself uneasily on the side of the skimmer just in time to look right into the second wave as it crashed down on both of us.

I do not know if the boat foundered at that point. I remember plunging headfirst over the left side and into the warm water—now menacing in its heat—and I felt a strange sucking sensation pulling my head under my body, almost spinning me into dizziness.

Oh no, came the thought, flashing through my mind like lightning. *A rip current.* In my periphery I could see the great blackness of the drop off that had been to my right before my fall. My brain reeled with misdirection, until I felt my back scrape against sand, and my mind reoriented itself. It was pulling me out to sea.

My leather diving suit gave me little in terms of maneuverability in water, and only with great effort did I manage to flip myself stomach-down and thrust my hand into the sand, thick tubes of air streaming from my nose and mouth.

That's when I saw it.

Only a foot or so to the left of my face stood the oblivion outline of curled lily petals. Time seemed to slow as my eyes followed the small coil of dulse seaweed to its origin at the center of the dark bloom.

It was beautiful, yet nothing like what I had seen before. The velvet petals were undoubtedly red, but they were deep, dark, and powerful in their umbral vibrance. The faintest sparkling of silvery purple highlighted their edges, but their filaments sank into a sable, infinite center, like a red brick well that continued for miles into the ground.

I screamed under the water, feeling the current pull my loose legs fiercely out to sea. Trying to bring them down to the ground, I clawed at the seafloor with both hands, dredging the sand into a flurry around me.

Just ten more centimeters . . . five . . . three.

I was overcome with the notion that I needed to touch it to really understand it. I clawed and clawed, and with one final lunge through the sucking sea, I was there. My two fingers, stretched to their limit, grazed the petals. With one last effort, my fingertips lightly hooked underneath them, around the flower.

Then it broke off. All of it. The dulse weed, the petals supported by the chasmic bulb, and the rich jet center all popped suddenly out of the sand. The last dregs of air in my lungs flew out to sea as my mouth hung open.

It was as if my mind couldn't comprehend that the roots of the lily didn't continue all the way to the center of the earth. I tried to grasp the fleeing flower with a feeble twist of my wrist, my limbs heavy and slow, but it slipped straight past my water-fettered arms and into the black abyss of the drop-off. I saw it only for a second more as its darkness stood out against the gray shadow of the sea. Then it was gone, diving beyond where the light of the midday sun could reach.

My last sensation before I too was ripped out into the coming tide was the release of my other hand, which had been buried in the sand. I don't remember being pulled from the water by René or him saving my life, though I was informed of the reality of this many times afterward. The only thing I do recall is a sudden realization I had after coughing up the water in my chest and finally breathing fresh air into my lungs: the realization that the dulse lily had been the most beautiful thing I had ever seen.

Of course, I did go back and try to find it. To this day, I remember the exact spot along the edge of the drop-off over which I witnessed it fall, and though there were countless clumps of seaweed and red-stained sand, the flower was gone, washed into oblivion. I spent the rest of my trip searching for and failing to find another specimen of the dulse lily. Even after staying for weeks more than I had planned, my efforts led only to more failure, and though my first attempts to find the flower were spurred on by a modicum of enthusiasm, I was quickly subdued by a presentment of sickness and lack of money. I do not have the strength or resources to return five years from now, nor am I sure that I would want to do so. Though I am writing this months after the encounter, the sea has not left my lungs. Sometimes, on particularly difficult days, I doubt it ever will. Coughs and fevers have a way of grinding a man down. I failed again. For the last time.

Letter addressed to Marco Arwaldt from Bixby Adams
Dresden University, Germany: Mailbox 24
February 14, 1834

Dear Mr. Arwaldt,

Congratulations! We are incredibly pleased to inform you that the manuscript you submitted has been accepted for publication. We have included a document that will need to be fully filled out by the author prior to the event, but we have gone ahead and preemptively added his work to the pending publishing list for you.

Unfortunately, our nearest manuscript is already being printed, but our upcoming "American Fiction Anthology" will, we think, be an excellent home for your manuscript. Submissions for it are due in June of this year.

Again, congratulations on your acceptance. We look forward to working with you and your client in the future.

Yours, Bixby Adams
Senior Editor
Clive Bros. Publishing

Letter addressed to Marco Arwaldt from James Torrey
Dresden University, Germany: Mailbox 24
April 20, 1834

Dear Marco,

I used to be enthralled with the beginnings of stories: that luster and depth which somehow springs from the beginning of a journey so soon to be embarked upon.

I had so much to see, so much to write. I could envision the pages upon pages of data, measurements, Latin names and titles — and I could imagine the esoteric beauty of a thirty-page reference section, stacked neatly in dotted layers, stamped into the perfectly cut pages by the printing press, and bound in a solid, hard brown cover.

Yet here I am now, at the end of my own journey, and I sadly don't remember having anywhere near the same amount of excitement at the beginning of these stories. That excitement, though still fleetingly present, was quickly eclipsed by the crushing weight of resolution, the barely bearable conflicts, and the inevitable end. The end to this story, which I have no choice but to present to you and whoever else might read this book, is all I have. My struggle has not entirely left me. My lungs still sting from the briny air, and my nerves lie shattered at the foot of my bed. I feel like I step on them every morning. I can barely write on the days that the neighbor's dogs bark too loud. I can only take short walks out into the sunny yards of what was my parents' farm. I can no longer tend the flowers.

But no more complaints. My book, at last, is finished, and at least it still has those beautiful images of the flowers that Amy drew. Perhaps in the future I will heal enough to garden, return to the beginning of my affair with flowers, and remember the light of those days when my mother would have me weed while she was busy. My adventures have swept me across the world, from the hot, damp forests of Asia to the frigid West of America. Laden with the burdens of these trips, I wonder if perhaps the blossoms I needed were not the rare colossi of the corpse flower or the resilient and fleeting blooms of the crown of spring, but the common tiny spirals of the lilac and the shining softness of the buttercup.

I have written many letters since my return: ones to you, to Swan, to Anisa, and a couple others. I still wait for Swan's reply in the mail, but I doubt Anisa's letter made it to Sumatra intact. Too many shipping lines and transfers, too many opportunities for errors to crop up. Really though, it is of no great importance if they receive them or not. The ones sent to those two mostly thank them for helping me with my book and tell them that if they had a reliable address, I would love to send them a copy. To Swan, I added an inquiry about his injured arm — as it was my fault in the end — and wished him and his family well. I ended by suggesting, half-jokingly, that against the backdrop of the whole world, we are not that far from each other, and a trip of a couple days could reunite us for a time once my health improves.

A failure, I see now, is what my account has become. That is the truth, and it is with a heavy pen that I share this. What I yearned for was undeniably a far goal bordering on the edge of the contemporary scientific landscape, but what I have in my hands, and what you now have in yours, is a packet of mixed words, a quasi-scientific pseudo-journal, stuck in the limbo between purpose and ludicrous passion. How funny it is, truly, that "close" isn't close to counting. A failure is all I can call it, and by proxy, myself.

Though I digress once again. Perhaps, at the conclusion of my trials and injuries, the truth is that there lies a great end somewhere here. Failures are just as complete as successes, are they not? And here, in my miniscity, my insufficiency, I conclude something that is much less than the razor-sharp scalpel of science. I can only present it to you, and hope that it is, at least, more than the sum of its parts.

I accept the offer of publication.

Letter addressed to James Torrey from Marco Arwaldt

Black Hawk, TN, USA

April 12, 1836

Dear James,

I write to you in excited haste. I have just received word from good friends over at the Hector Institute that they have found your flower! Can you believe it? What an incredible feat of modern botanical science, and all because of you. I inquired personally by post what led them to the discovery, and they unabashedly cited your manuscript as a defining source of locational focus. Of course, we were a little off the mark originally, but your diligence in Mauritius was undoubtedly responsible for the inception of their expedition.

I am writing with hopes that you will join me to view the specimen recovered from the island. The flower is being closely guarded by the Institute since it is such a rare species, but I have managed to convince them, due to your pioneering work in the field, that you should be able to see it again. They eagerly accepted after hearing I knew you personally, and we have an hour-long window for our appointment in Gloucester just a few months from me sending this letter. I have already made arrangements for you to board a ship in New York on the fifteenth of July. The details are enclosed. I will pick you up by carriage from the port when you arrive, and I have friends in the city that can accommodate us for the few days in between.

Let me know whether or not you plan to come, although I must admit I will be very sad if your reply is in the negative. It has been too long, my friend — over two years at this point. I can't wait to see you again.

Sincerely yours,
Marco

Letter posted on the 12th of December, 1836

Received from sender by PO clerk at Black Hawk, US Post Office.

Destination: Not applicable

Sender: Mr. James E. Torrey
Return Address: 312 Pate Ln., Black Hawk, Tennessee
Postage Paid: Yes
Our for Delivery: Not applicable

Status: UAA (Undeliverable as Addressed). Redirected by local DLO.

Dear Amy,

I know I will not send this. I cannot send this — I have nowhere to send it to. How ridiculous, but through some caving-in of my own thought I have decided that this is important. I have thought too much on the topic I'm about to share and have come to that conclusion. It is inane, I know. You will not read this — perhaps ever — but it is still important to me, at least, that I write this last part of my journey down. That it gets out of my head and onto the page, any page.

It is also important, somehow — for some strange, ineffable reason that I do not have the power to impart — that I write this to you.

Here it is.

The last of it.

*

I was there, sitting at the foot of the massive brick building of the Hector Institute only two years after my final failure in Mauritius. Marco was at my side, his tall figure blocking the radiant winter sun.

"Our appointment is in half an hour still. Would you like to walk through the town for a bit?" he asked, rotating his head to the left to look at me without moving his shadow. I couldn't make out his features through the dark fog of his silhouette. I didn't answer. I found that I had been caught in a strange haze the whole morning and was having difficulty extracting myself from it, even to talk to Marco. He had obviously noticed. I felt the heavy weight of his open palm as he patted me on the shoulder.

"I'll go inside and ask if they are ready for us."

I still couldn't see his face. He left my side and strode powerfully toward the building, leaving me out in the sun. He had perfected the art of walking in a dignified manner without the prop of a paper case or cane during his tenure at Dresden. It was as if he crossed the distance of almost ten meters in three domineering strides.

I drifted to the right and sat down on a short backless wooden bench facing away from the entrance to the botanical institute. Absentmindedly, my hand rubbed my shoulder, searching for something to do. I wasn't sure why my feelings weren't as excited as they should have been. I had started the day practically bouncing on my heels. I had dressed quickly while my memory of the *palmaria* resurfaced over and over in my mind: its silky black petals, its unplumbed depths, were still vivid in my memory.

But, as we called our cab and began riding westward toward the research facility, that memory had started to fade. The short blips of images started to shimmer and vibrate under my recollecting mind's eye. I tried to conjure them back again, focus harder on one aspect or another, but they disintegrated even further under my mental gaze. This haze mounted to a peak when we arrived at our destination, and as I stepped out of the carriage, the memory had all but disappeared.

It was a Sunday, and the Hector Institute was closed to the public. The curator of the building had made an exception for us, however, and promised to open it up for an hour to allow us a view of the captured flower.

Marco had tried to talk to me, walking kindly in step, but I was so focused on my fading vision that it was all I could do to answer with simple statements or affirmations. It was as if each word jarred my brain and dislodged the imaginary frame I was trying to build.

Now, as I sat on the bench, the picture still eluded me. Behind me, the idea of the Hector Institute loomed over my hunched form. Its vivid red brick closed off the flower, locking it far away. The interior had been lit up for us, shining and incandescent. I didn't look at it. Instead my gaze wandered up toward the English sky.

It was a windy day; the breeze parsed its way through the buildings. Above I could see the slow passage of wolf-gray clouds. The sky was a deep blue and was jaggedly interrupted by the uneven horizon of the surrounding buildings. The tops of the connected flats stuck out at diagonal angles, flaring their silhouettes out all along the skyline. It looked like it would rain in the afternoon.

My eyes sunk down toward the street. The sidewalk across from the bench was cracked and crumbling. Its small fractures crept down to the red cobblestone road. I followed the crack as it progressed across the street; it had apparently been caused by an overarching fault in the ground underneath, as it permeated the barriers between different stones and packed dirt. The crack widened as it got closer to me, spreading from barely a centimeter in width to six-times that.

As my eyes followed it to my feet, I felt a hand on my shoulder again.

"They are ready for us," Marco said.

I startled out of my observation, my body almost rising from its spot, but as the action started, my legs froze up and rooted me to the spot. I sank back down, still staring forward.

"I think I'll just stay here for a little bit longer," I said without shifting focus.

I heard a slight inhale of surprise from Marco, and his hand twitched off my shoulder as I fell back down to the bench. I saw his thumb curl ponderously between his pointer and middle fingers.

After a second of silence, Marco exhaled and relieved the pressure of action entirely by sitting down beside me, also facing away from the Institute and toward the sun. I could see his face now out of the corner of my eye.

"I must confess, I caught a glimpse of it as we walked by. What an incredible specimen. Some of the dulse has deteriorated with the moving process, but it is my understanding that they have cultivated more and plan to introduce it into the growing environment to affect the flower's development. I'm not really sure if that's true. Such a process seems scientifically ridiculous when one considers . . ."

He trailed off. I knew his head had turned and he was regarding me, though I couldn't bring myself to meet his gaze. After a second of uncomfortable waiting, I took a deep breath in and glanced in his direction.

He had returned to looking straight ahead as I had been, his eyes squinting over the top of his glasses. The sun came out quickly from behind a passing cloud and shined in his face, forcing him to use their rims to shadow his pupils.

A full minute must have passed.

"It . . . it really is a beautiful flower," he said at last.

To my great surprise, a laugh bubbled out of my mouth. I covered it quickly with my hand and swallowed it down, embarrassed and shocked.

I looked over at Marco to apologize. He looked as surprised as I was. His eyebrow was raised almost comically above one eye, and his mouth wore a tightly closed smile as if he were trying not to laugh as well.

The strange silence was broken. We talked, though not about the flower, or the curator who was ostensibly waiting for us inside, but about . . . other things.

About Anisa. About China. About Swan. Even about you.

The fog ebbed away, inch by inch, until my memory slid back into view. The *Lilium palmaria* slowly materialized again as if my mind was a microscope being refocused.

The minutes passed as we faced the street. The conversation wandered in some places and fell away in others.

Our allotted time period slipped past slowly.

Ten minutes past the start time . . .

Twenty . . .

Thirty-five . . .

Forty-seven . . .

Then it had been an hour and a half . . . Two hours.

Three times the amount of our appointment passed in this way, and I hardly noticed. Sometimes we just sat in silence, watching the sun drip between the building tops.

Eventually, after the shadows reached across the intersecting road, I looked behind me. The lights had all been turned off. The incandescent interior of the building had faded back to a black shadow.

I caught a glimpse of Marco as I turned back to face the skyline. He had one leg crossed over the other, and had propped his elbow up on his knee, leaning forward to rest his chin on his palm. Another minute passed.

Out of the corner of my eye, I saw Marco's nose crinkle above his curled fingers, and I could tell that he was smiling. He took a deep breath, uncrossed his legs, and rose silently to his feet. I understood but stayed and stared for a moment more — not back at the building, but up at the gray sky, clouded and tall. Marco did too, the clement wind pressing his coat against the back of his legs. It had indeed started to rain gently.

Finally, I rose too, and pushed by the momentum of the eastward breeze, we left.

194

Letter posted on the 3rd of November, 1837

Received from courier by PO clerk at Black Hawk, US Post Office.

Destination: To Jamie Torrie
312 Pate Ln., Black Hawk, Tennessee

Sender: No name given
Return Address: Not applicable
Postage Paid: Yes
Out for Delivery: November 30, 1837

Status: Delivered